THE NUT CRACKER

Eric Lynch

RoseDog Books

PITTSBURGH, PENNSYLVANIA 15222

ISBN # 0-8059-9724-5
Printed in the United States of America

First Printing

For additional information or to order additional books,
please write:
RoseDog Publishing
701 Smithfield Street
Pittsburgh, Pennsylvania 15222
U.S.A.
1-800-834-1803
Or visit our web site and on-line bookstore at
www.rosedogbookstore.com

My name is 'Jim Sears, I am twenty-one years old, five feet eleven and a half inches tall. I am a very quiet person.

My parents thought me to mind my own business, but not to take crap from anyone.

That I should respect the law, and keep out of trouble, also respect other people and there rights, irrespective of their nationality, color, culture, or country of birth.

IT ALL STARTED WITH A KNOCK ON MY BED ROOM DOOR, EARLY ONE VERY COLD November morning.

In another thirty minutes, I would be up and on my way to work.

Instead I was looking at my land lord standing at my bed room door, with another gentleman; dress in a dark shabby grey suit. His suit was wet, and looks like it had seen better days.

He was a big man; a rough estimate, height six feet six, weight three hundred pounds or more, age forty-five to fifty years old, receding hair line makes him looks a lot older.

The first thing that caught my eyes was his feet as I open the door looking down, still half a sleep, I could not miss his large feet. Looking up I could see from the reaction on his face, he knew I was looking at them. The son of a bitch, have large feet I thought as I yawn.

Then my land lord voice disturb my though. 'This is he started to say.'

But before he couldn't finish what he was about to say, because the big man said will you come down stairs sir.

Why, who are you? "The police my land lord said quickly, finishing what he started to say."

What the hell for I ask? Why are you getting me out of bed this early? Instead of telling me why, he repeats will you come down stairs please.

This time he made it sound very urgent.

Again I ask why? And again he repeats come down stairs sir.

I did not like anyone waking me up; because I am not an early morning person, so I was not in a good mood, and I knew the big man sense this.

1

"Come down stairs sir, he said again." Looking at his face, tells me he was not an early morning person either, and would not take no for an answer. "Get dress or put your dressing gown on, and a pair of slippers he said."

Telling me what I should do, did not go down very well either.

His voice sounds like he was giving me an order, and not a request.

He made it looks like I could not think for myself, and for a brief moment I felt like I was back in the army again.

Standing there, I could feel the cold coming from down stairs.

I could also see it was rain, through the window on the landing; and this tells me it was not a nice morning.

You know the type of morning one should stay in bed. It was the second week in November, and the house was very cold.

My land lord did not think he should put the heating on at night, when you are in bed you are warm he would say, so there is no need to warm the house.

To be honest, he thought it was a crime to put the heating on anytime day or night, it had to freeze before he would put it on.

And then the only reason he would put it on, is because he was afraid the water pipes would freeze, and if it freezes he would only put it on for a few hours at night.

I want to go and live in a warmer country before I get old he would say, telling us this as often as he could, and why he was saving every penny he got hold of.

He did not care how cold the house got, because he kept is bed room warm, and that's where he spends most of his time.

If you're cold in your room that is your problem, he often says he made allowance for heating in the rent.

I thought it was just an excuse to get his tenants to keep the house worm for him.

As I step back into my room, and start to close the door big foot said, the house is surrounded sir.

I open the door again, and look at him very serious and say, I am bloody one floor up, and I have not develop the ability to fly yet.

Looking at his face once again I could see my remark did not go down very well.

My land lord looks at my face and said, "Jim, this won't take long," he said again very quickly as if that would make it right.

2

I hesitate, then look at him for at least thirty second, then I said this better be good.

Looking back at big foot, again I get the impression this man is not an early morning person, either.

From the way he was looking at me, this made me very angry, and I knew he knew it.

Down stairs there were two gentlemen, one with scraggly grey hair, and a thick grey moustache, his grey eye brows was as thick as his moustache, and long and bushy. His pale blue eyes, looks very sickly, and he was coughing a lot.

His black coat was much two large for him; and I could see he was not warm, because he was trembling as he stood in the centre of the room.

With very deep wrinkles on his face he had the type of face; you would call a live in face,

You know the type of face that say I have seen it all, or think he's seen it all.

But worse of all he was old, and looks like he could do with a good night sleep.

With all the blood drain from his face, this leaves him looking a pale and dingy, with sickly grey complication

He looks very tired and scared, I am sure if I shout boo, he would run out the door faster than a cat.

The other gentleman, dress in a blue wrinkled suit that was also looking a bit wet, it looks as if he went to sleep in it.

His black shoes needed cleaning, but I could see a few rain drops on them even though they were dirty.

He also looks like he could climb into my bed that was still warm.

It was plain to see he was the other police officer; because he had a serious look on his face, the type of look that leaves me feeling even colder.

With both men staring at me, as I enter the sitting room, I felt this will not be good news.

But at least the room felt a little warmer than the stairs.

I was "surprise" to see that the land lord lit the gas fire for them.

I thought that must be breaking his little heart.

The big man who came down the stairs behind me asks is this the man sir?" Yes the grey hair old man said. "That's him."

3

Him, what I ask? "Turn your back and put your hands on you head now, the policeman in front said," without moving from beside the old man who move closer to him.

I did not turn; instead I look from one to the other, and then at my landlord.

I stood there lost for words, as if frozen to the spot where I stood.

It was as if someone suddenly took my brain away, everything went blank.

Big foot was still behind me.

Suddenly he grabs my arms and twists them up my back; this made me cry out in pain.

He was forcing my arms up the center my back as far as they would go, just to put the cuffs on.

I was crying out you are hurting me. But he took no notice.

He knew he was hurting me, and I had the feeling he was enjoying it, because he put the cuffs on as tight as he could.

This made me bend over so far, my head was almost touching my knees.

While he was doing that, the other officer starts to read me my rights.

I was shock and in so much pain, I could not hear what he was saying.

You are hurting me I shout. What have I done? No one answered.

What the hell did I do? I shout even louder. "You will find out later someone said."

The grey hair old man, mumbled something as he move away, as far as he could move in the small room.

When he was sure he was far enough away he said, "My wife will recognize him officer."

"She saw him."

"Ok sir you can bring her down to the station later."

The other officer who read me my rights turns to my land lord, and asks how long have you known what his name? "His name is 'Jim, officer, he moved into the room," it will be four weeks tomorrow officer." Did he tell you where he came from? "No officer." How did he pay the rent the first time? "He paid cash officer."

Did he pay one week or two weeks? "He paid two weeks officer."

Did you say two weeks? "Yes he paid two weeks officer."

Do you make it a habit renting to strangers? He did not answer.

4

Do you at least know where he is from? "No officer."
Did you ask him? "No officer."
The only thing I can say about you 'Mr. Lacus, you are a very trusting man.
Do you have a key to his room? "No officer," Jim, has the key."
"Can I have the key?" It's up stairs.

These cuffs are hurting my wrist I said. They took no notice.
Instead he asks where I was from. So I took no notice.
"Did you hear me he?" Yea I heard you; these cuffs are hurting my wrist I said, did you hear me.
He stood there, looking at me as if I was not in the room.
"Let's go and get the key," and you can get dress at the same time big foot said."
As we walk up stairs my knee's felt weak, I felt like I was going to pass out.
Why are you arresting me? He did not answer.

What you are arresting me for I ask again; please tell me what I done.
He still did not answer.
I repeat my question again, he still ignores me, I stop, and he pushes me very hard, I slip and fell forward, but I did not hit the floor, I manage to save myself.
I stood there refusing to move. "Look, I am very tired he said," so don't you push me two far if you know what's good for you."

"Because of you I lost a night sleep," so move your sorry ass up those stairs," you half breed son of a bitch, I am not going to tell you again."
"So if you know what's good for you move, now and keep going?" For a brief moment I was thinking I'll throw myself backwards on him.
Then I thought with my hands in handcuffs behind me, I may break my back or worse my neck.

So I took a deep breathe and walk slowly up the stairs. He followed me into my room, and removes one wrist from the handcuff, and watches me dress.
When I finish, he grab my arm and put the cuffs on again.
He did not let me have a wash or comb my hair.
He took my keys off the night table without asking for it, and locks the door as we walk out; then put the keys in his pocket.
Down stairs he said to my landlord no one goes into that room.

We walk out to the car and I get in, in the police station, big foot said book him please 'Don, and walk away.

Don took me into a small room, pull a chair out from under a table. "Sit he said."

As we sat at the table I said the cuffs, is hurting my wrist.

I was surprised he removes them.

Full name please he said.

What did I do I ask? Why are you arresting me? "Full name please he said again?" And again I ask what I did.

"This is the last time I am going to ask you what is your name."

Well go and screw yourself, I want to know what the hell you are arresting me for? "He said nothing, but his face went bright red, as he stood up.

"You think this is funny, I'll ask you again what your name is?" To hell with you, can't you fucking hear? When you tell me what I did, and why I am here, then I may answer your questions.

I reach the stage where I did not care, I had nothing to drink or eat, and I did nothing wrong, I could do with a wash and shave, so as far as I was concern, they may as well lock me up and throw the keys away.

Look I done nothing to be treated the way I am been treated I shout.

Don got up and leaves the room.

When he came back big foot came with him.

"Looking at me he said you broke into the corner shop," and you threaten the shop keeper and his wife with a machete, and you took all there money."

"Now you know what you fucking did." You must be fucking mad I shout.

Well a black man with a machete woke them up; and you fit the description, does that answer your entire question."

He was very calm when he said it; there was no sign of uncertainty on his voice.

Once again I froze, I could not believe what I was he haring, it was as if someone hit me on my head with a brick.

My blood was rushing so fast to my head, I could hear my heart beating in my ears, and at the same time I could feel it pounding in my chest so hard it felt as if it was trying to get out.

"We search your room, and we fond three hundred pounds in your suitcase; you are in big trouble."

"Where did you get that money?" Its mine, I did not steal it.

The officer in the blue suit walks in, and 'Don, leave the room.

If you are arresting me I know my rights, I need a lawyer.

Big foot looks at me but took no notice.

Instead he carries right on telling me about the shop. "The shop is very close to where you live aren't it." It is very handy, it is in the right place to nip in and out quickly, and you're home and dry."

What do you take me for? I am not that stupid, do you think I am so stupid I shit on my own door step.

"Meaning what he asks?" Well I said if you "don't" want the flies to come into the house, you don't shit on your door steps do you? "Are you calling me a fly?" Well you said it, I did not.

"You think you are a clever son of a bitch," don't you?" I told you I am tired, so I am going to say this one more time, what is your name?" I did not answer.

"I don't have time to waste with you, so answer my fucking questions now, if you know what's good for you." I did not answer.

"For the last time what is your full name he shouts close to my ear?" I will give you my name when my lawyer is here.

Big foot got up, and stood as close as he could at the back of my chair.

I could see from the expression on his face he was mad, his face went from pale white to deep red in seconds.

"You son of a bitch, he shouts, you don't hear so good do you?" Suddenly he grabbed the back of my chair, and pushes me and the chair right across the room; with such force the chair hit the wall on the other side of the room, as it did, I toppled on the floor.

Before I could get up, he was standing above me looking down at me shouting, "I don't have to take you and your crap." "Who the fuck do you thing think you are?" I try to stand up; with by back close to the wall, when I was almost up he punches me so hard in my gut, I felt my back hit the wall.

It was as if his fist went right through me and hit the wall, I felt my ribs crack.

Falling to the floor breathless, and gasping for air, as I roll around on the floor, I could hear him shouting, get up you son of a bitch, and tell me your name.

As I lay there gasping for breathe for quite a while, I caught glimpses of his feet as he circle the room like a mad man.

Then after a while he came back and stood above me again, still shouting what is your name, "I want your name."

I try to get up again, but could hardly get up.

Get up he shouts, still standing very close to me, so close I was looking at his private, while on my knees, I close my fist and hit him as hard as I could in his testicles.

And I watch all six feet six and a half inches of big foot fall down on his knees beside me and roll on his side, holding his balls.

As he lay beside me gasping for breath, I hit him again in his gut as hard as I could, and roll away from him shouting if you are going to kill me, take that to remember me you bastard. I don't care what you are, or who you are, you do not have the right to hit me, so fuck you.

His partner came rushing around the table and grab my arm, as I was about to hit him again.

Pulling me away with such force, I was thrown right across the other side of the room again.

This time hitting my head on the wall, with blood poor out of my nose, as I wipe it away everything went blank.

The next thing I remember is waking up in hospital, with a cop in uniform sitting beside my bed.

As I open my eyes, he calls for the nurse. She looks at me, and calls the doctor.

"I am doctor 'Weisberg, don't try to talk or move about two much he said."

"You have two broken ribs, and a fractured your skull," so stay very still."

I was still mad; get him out of here doc, I said pointing at the officer.

"Will you wait out side please officer?" I am sorry doc no, my orders is to stay by his bed.

"I am in charge here will you please wait out side the door," he won't be going anywhere."

"I am sure he can't fly, we are three floors up, and that door is the only door out of this room."

"Now will you wait out side the door?" He still hesitates.

Doctor Weisberg stood his ground, and stares at him, as he walk away slowly, saying I will call this in."

You can do that, but please go now, and wait out side the door."

Checking to see that I was alright, he gave me an injection, this will keep you calm.

Everyday I saw a different doctor.

They all took a quick look at me and leave, saying nothing.

Five days after the beating, two men smartly dress, came in with doctor 'Weisberg.

They stood by my bed.

"This is detective 'Nelsons, and detective 'Duncan,' they want a word with you."

"If you have any problem please ring the bell."

"Nelson, tall with a "permanent" smirk on his face looking some what like a smile, he had thick eye brows, big ears, and a dimple in his chin you can't miss, because that's the first thing your eyes see, apart from his big ears.

He stood there looking very sure of himself, I could see he was a born leader; I could also tell from the tone of his voice as soon as he starts asking me questions.

And right away I got the feeling he thinks he is it, and I am shit.

So I whisper to myself, here is another one who wants my skin, and for the first time in my life I knew I was in trap, and it felt like the walls were closing in on me, and there was no way out.

So I sat very still and say nothing, just in case I say something he could use on me later.

'Duncan, chubby with graying black hair, with an over size moustache, and a face that looks like it seen better days, but it was still searching for something he can't find.

When he walks across to my bed, he looks like was gliding, he is a real little darling I thought.

I could see from the expression on his face, he would like to skin me given half a chance. Looking straight at him, I said you would like to skin me right now, wouldn't you? You would like to hang me on the wall right here to dry wouldn't you? He did not answer,

Instead he stares at me, as if to say you are lucky I can't get my hands on you.

'Okay' doc, we will take it from here. "Nelson said," and pull the chairs close to my bed. Sitting down his first words were, "you are in big trouble; you are knee deep in shit."

9

Okay if that is what you have to tell me, there is the door, I do not wish to hear anymore.

You walk in here, and right away I am in trouble, you decide that I am guilty without a trial, well there is the blasted doors go I said again.

"That is not the way 'Duncan, said."

So since you are so clever you tell me the way? You meet me for the first time and right away I am in trouble right up to my ass.

The both of you found me guilty as soon as you walk through the door, didn't you. He said nothing.

What are you waiting for; tell me what the way is? I lay there waiting but got no answer. Well if you want to know, this is what happens to me, two assholes got me out of bed; very early, cold and hungry, they drag me down to the flea pit, you call a police station, they did not let me have a wash, or clean my teeth.

At the station they did not give me a hot drink; even though it was as cold as hell, they treat me like you would not treat your dog, and then they accuse me of breaking into a shop up the street, and if that was not enough, he beat the crap out of me.

"Beat you?" Yes who the hell do you think put me here? You got to be stupid, if you think I crack my own skull, I am sure I don't look that stupid.

Man I am so stupid I bash my head in the wall, hell I bet you think I should let that son of a bitch, beat the crap out of me, and that I should sit there and take it.

Well I have news for you this is one guy that will always fight back every time; I will never bend over for anyone.

I pause took a deep breath; as they sat there looking at me.

Detective 'Duncan, break the silence. "You must obey the law he said again."

Come off it, there you go again; what you are telling me is, if two men come into your house, get you out of your warm bed, handcuff you, and drag you to the police station, and then tell you, you broke into a shop up the road, then beat the crap out of you, because you won't give them your name, is that the law.

Well if that's the law, open the fucking cell door; I am "coming in.

I don't need a trial; just sling the fucking key away once I am in.

"I warning you watch your language detective 'Nelson, said snapping at me." Don't warn me you are wasting your time.

10

"Who the hell do you think you are 'Duncan, said?" Look I said, if it pleases you, you can come and beat the crap out of me everyday, but don't expect me to sit and take it, law or no law.

So please do me, a favor tell all those bastards who want to beat me, to be very careful because I'll give more than I get.

"You are one cheeky son of a bitch that's for sure, 'Duncan, mumbled, just loud enough for me to hear."

Do you want to know something I said? You are fucking right; I said it just loud enough for him to hear.

Then I ask him out loud so anyone could hear, do you feel like breaking some ribs? Help yourself; I have a lot more, and I am in the hospital, so it will be alright.

I don't have far to go, so help yourself, break some more. His face start to get red; he stood up, and sit down again, then stood up and walk towards the door.

After a few minutes he came back, and he sat down, for the umpteen times. I said to him, you have a big problem, and I don't care a shit.

Do you want to know why? "Go on tell me why he said."

I know, you know the only thing anyone can do to me, is beat the crap out of me.

And there is a limit to that, because if I fight back hard enough somebody may kill me.

And that son of a bitch will be up for the high jump.

I maybe in big trouble now, but it could get worse.

I will tell you this, when you are all finish, my lawyers will have a field day.

Goodbye, see you when the doctors release me.

"Who is leaving?" You are, no both of you. 'Ha, ha very funny 'Duncan, said.'

"Do you want to you know something he said?" You talk two much."

Well, I am only telling you as it is, and how it will be, I' won't let you are anyone change me.

Nor will I kiss anyone's ass.

They kept asking questions, one first then the other.

I totally ignore them; it took them quite a while before they realize, I was not going to say any more.

11

"Then 'Nelson said, you better get a good lawyer, you will need one."
Looking at you can't afford one."

Ha, well that means I don't stand a chance do I? So why don't you lock
me up and throw away the key right now.

Open the door quick here I come; I'll make it easy for you I will walk
in.

"I can see you are not in the mood to talk Nelson said." It's the first
sensible thing you said since you came in.

"So if I can say something that makes some sense, why cant you?"
Nelson said.

"Let's finish this discussion in the station, when you are out it will be
better for all of us."

"Believe me you will be glad to tell us every thing you know." So tell
me Mr. Nelson how are you going to get me to tell you everything I know?
He said nothing.

A few days later, a police officer came, with a prison uniform, and hand
it to me.

"Get dress now he said."

I took my time, "hurry up he said." I took no notice.

Then another cop came in, "put our hands on your head he said."

I stood there, like I heard nothing. "Are you deaf?" I stood there and
ignore him.

I watch his face get red? "I was told about you he said." I hope am living up to your expectations I said? "So you will both have something, you
can tell your mothers and wives when you get home."

Just then the doctor walks in, he did not say anymore. See you soon
doc.

"Why?" I doubt if I will get back to the station without a beating.

"Doc he is a nice one, don't you think?" He thinks everyone wants to
beat him.

It took them a while before they realize; I was not doing what they ask,
so he walk behind me took one of my arms and gently pull it behind me,
and then the other arm and put the hand cuffs on.

When we got to the car he open the door, get in be quick about it he
said, leaving me in no doubt that if I did not do as he ask he would hit me.

I was now out of site of the hospital so I get in, because my broken ribs
were still hurting.

At the station no one said anything to me; they took me straight to a cell, and bang I heard the door slam behind me, as it slam I felt like screaming so I quickly put my hand over my mouth to muffle the scream.

Next day, they walk into the cell put your hands on your head the copper said, nothing else, so I said no.

"Put your god dam hands on top of your head he said again." No I said again.

I don't want any trouble he said so I will do it for you.

He walks behind me and put the hand cuffs on.

It was the same routine; everyday they took me for questioning, and the questions was always the same, and my answer was the same.

When am I going to see a lawyer? "Can't you learn a different tune Nelson asks?" Not the one you would like me to sing, that's for sure, I said.

Every time they came for me; it was always the same. Stand up they would say, and I remain seated, and they would help me up, and put the cuff on.

Where are we going this time I ask? "We are not going out, that's for sure he said."

"Ha, ha very funny, we have a funny one today, are you always that funny I ask? He did not answer.

We walk into a little room, sit the officer said and walk out.

'Nelson, and 'Duncan, walks in, and sits down, where have you been I ask? I thought you were in a hurry to see me.

I thought you would come to see me much sooner.

They said nothing; they just sat there looking at the papers they bought in, leaf by leaf, as I watch them turn the pages, as if they have not read them before.

After a while, they both look at me all most together.

You are in big trouble now boy, boy you're trouble run through my mind as they read.

"Officer 'Gurney, is badly hurt; Nelson said. 'We can't have this.' 'We can't have you assaulting our officers can we."

Who is 'Gurney I ask? There was a long silence.

After a while I said you mean big foot, man it's all right for him to break my ribs, and crack my skull, can you have that? Well I have news for you I can't have that either.

13

That will teach the son of a bitch that he can't beat up everyone, tell him there is always someone who will fight back, tell him I hope he will get better soon. I said mockingly.

Enough about him when am I going to see a lawyer? I have nothing to say to you lot, without a lawyer present. They stood up.

Here we go again I thought this is it; they are going to beat the crap out of me again.

I was surprise when they walk out of the door; I did not expect this, because no matter, who came to question me I ignore them, or ask for my lawyer, and they always get nasty, and threaten me.

Sitting there for a long time the door slowly open, I was looking down at my legs under the table.

I was getting cramp in the right leg, and my wrist was hurting.

Once again they put on the hand cuff tight; somehow I think they do this on purpose.

So when the door opens I did not look up, even though, there was a slight smell of perfume in the room.

Looking under the table I could see a pair of neat little shoe, with narrow toes, and stiletto heels and a very slender pair of legs.

The slight whiff of perfume got stronger as she came close to the table; it was not over powering, it was just enough to tell me she was there.

As I slowly raise my eyes taking in the view, I thought who ever own those legs and that figure must also have a nice face.

As I slowly work my way to her face, I was not "disappointed." Wow came to my lips as my mouth fell open, I whisper to myself put your tongue back in boy.

I whisper so loud she heard me.

'That is a good idea she said.'

Her long brunette hair hangs over her shoulders; it was almost down to her waist.

Her full red lips invite me to look into her hazel eyes, her nice tan olive skin, told me she just came back from a sunshine holiday.

I thought hell she must look stunning in a bikini.

A quick estimate, height five eight or nine, with a 36-22-36 figure; I sat there lost for words as she looks at me.

'I am your lawyer she said; with a very soft voice and a faint smile on her lips,' that seems to say I am it and you're shit. You're what? "Your lawyer she said again."

What the hell are you talking about? "I am appointed by the courts."

To do what I asks? If you don't mind I'll choose my own lawyer, I don't know you.

Did they choose you because you are in their back pockets? When they pull the strings did you jump out of your pretty little box, and shout I will do it. I will help you to put him down? 'Let's put you right, my name is 'Lisa Myrna, I am no ones puppet; and I pull my own strings, she said with an angry frown across her brows.

"The choice is yours she said; find your own lawyer, if that's what you want and start closing the folder she opened."

'Okay' I said lets hear what you have to say? "Don't do me any favors she said." I am not.

So for a start let's forget everything that is written in that folder.

Hear me first, because if they told you what you have written in your folder it is all lies.

She closes it, and put it down on the table.

'Looks at me, let's hear it, lets hear your side as you put it.'

For starters I am innocent; I did not break into that shop.

"Can you prove it she asks?" Can you prove you were a sleep in your bed last night I ask? If no one saw you before you went to bed? Or see you in bed.

Or worse can you prove you did not get up in the night? Went out and break into a shop, just up the road from where you live.

She said nothing; instead she opens the folder again. Are you obsessed with that folder I ask? She did not answer. She looks at me and wrote something in it.

When she finishes writing, she looks straight at me, eyes wide open, without a blink, she said, leave me, to do my job or I walk out the door.'

"I must ask this question did you break into the shop."

Still looking at me waiting for an answer, I look at her with disbelief; I just told her I am innocence.

We look at each other for a while before she realizes, I was not going to answer her. Then she said, 'I can see from your face, that question disturbs you.'

'Is that the question, 'detective,' I cut her short, before she could say his name? Let's call him big foot.

Or better yet, from now on we will call them detective big foot, and partner.

I do not wish to hear his name, the less I hear his name, the better off I will be.

"You better get use to hearing his name, because you will be hearing a lot about him in court." I was still staring at her looking very serious.

"Ok" big foot and partner, it is for now she said."

'What question did they ask you?' And why did you attack them?' I attack them. Ha, ha that's a laugh.

Where did you get that from? Is that the story they are telling? I bet he did not tell you if his balls survive a direct hit. With every ounce of power I could muster up, with two broken ribs.

I hit the son of a bitch dead centre between his crotches as hard as I could while on my knees.

I bet the son of a bitch can't use his balls.

I bet he has to think before he can sit or piss.

I am sure he will have to do everything with care for while.

I bet I spoil quite a few of his weekends, I said laughing at my remarks.

What I said did not offend her; instead she just kept on writing.

But I could see a slight smile on her lips, even though; she tries her best to hide it.

She looks up; flip her head to the right, to remove her long hair away from her face.

Then she picks it up with her long fingers, and put it behind her ears, and over her shoulder.

Man I thought that's nice, she did it so neat with her fingers it sends a tingle down my spine.

When she look up at me again, there was a long pause, before she wrote some more. While I sat there admiring her beauty, her long slender fingers, the shape of her nose, lips, and her long eye lashes.

The slight smell of perfume all around the room was slowly consuming me.

She stops writing, and look at me again.

Then look down and start writing again.

May I ask a question I said? Almost in a whisper like a little school boy who is unsure of himself. "By all means she said."

Looking up at me for a few second, and look down at the folder and start writing again.

Are you sure I ask? "Yes she said."

I pause for a while.

She looks up waiting for me to ask.

I look into her eyes, wondering if I dare ask.

16

Thinking about my question for a quite a while, as she sat there looking at me, waiting very patiently, 'then she said what you want to know?' I thought what the hell can she do, she can't eat me "that's" for sure.

What is it like going to bed with you? God it must be like dying and going to heaven on earth, I said smiling.

Her face went blood red; her exposed ear went even redder.

Her eyes gave her away, they sparkle, with pride. I could see she did not expect that type of question.

I waited for an answer; it took her a while to find it. "I am sorry she said,' in a very soft spoken voice, sounding almost like a little young girl. "You'll never know."

'Ha, well there is no harm in dreaming is there, I said.

"As long as you don't have nightmares she said," still blushing.

Well I said, if "that's" the only way I can find out, I hope I have one tonight.

I could see that she was now caught with her guard down; she was not as sure as she was when she first walks through the door.

Suddenly we were not talking about me that made her feel very uneasy, she start to fidget in her chair.

And spend a lot more time brushing her hair back with her fingers.

The way she was moving around on her chair, it was as if she was sitting on something hot. Suddenly she stood up.

Why are you running away just when I was getting to know you? I am not running away.

Please stay a while longer, I promise I will not ask you anymore questions like that.

"Sorry I must leave, I have another appointment, but I'll be back to see you again."

Very soon I hope.

With a smile on her face, she walks slowly towards the door.

'Ha well there goes all my dreams; I said, she pauses at the door and look back, with a big smile.

As the door open and shut behind her, nice butt I whisper to myself.

Then the pains suddenly return to my arms, with a cramp feeling running up to my shoulders and down my fingers.

The handcuffs were so tight there was no feeling in my fingers.

When I return to my cell, my brain start to run wild, over all the things that is happen to me the pass few days.

17

For the first time I wonder when this "nightmare" will end.

I did not have a nightmare or dream of 'Lisa, but I could not get her out of my mind.

I don't know why she leaves such a deep impression on me.

Some people would call it love at first sight; I don't believe that is possible, at least not for me.

I tried very hard to think what will happen to me,' but came up against a brick wall all night; because no matter what I did I could only think of her.

I ask myself what the hell she would want me for; I have nothing, and branded a thief.

In another life maybe she would look at me.

It would be much easer for me to fill a bucket with a hole, than get her in bed.

I spend the next two day in the sell, with all my meals push through the little hole in the door.

Walking, around in circle over and over, for something to do.

For the first time, I know what a wild animal feels like, going round and round, in a circle with no where to go.

Suddenly I stop going round, and whisper to myself, those poor animals, done nothing wrong, just like me lock-up for nothing. I got very; very angry, so angry tears came to my eyes. I sat in that cell for two more days.

Only catching a glimpse of someone face, pushing my food through the little hole, in the door. Then one day the door open.

The first voice I heard for days, said turn your back, face the wall put your hands on your head. I did nothing.

He walks behind me and put the cuffs on, and he gave me a push move.

When I enter the room detective 'Nelson, and 'Duncan, was sitting there, with there folders on the table. "Sit was the first word 'Duncan, said."

This hand cuff is two tight; I said. There was no response from them.

They just look at me with blank faces, as if I was not in the room. So I said it again.

I waited and still got no response from them.

This hand cuff is two tight I repeat, saying it louder; there was still no "response. So I fart as loud as I could, it was one of my best farts; the spell was second to none,' and it fills the room very quick.

They grab their nose, got up very quick and ran to the door leaving it, open.

Hello I shout as they ran, it's nice to know you are both alive. After a while they came back.

Are you back for more I ask? They stood there and look at me; 'you are one discussing son of a bitch 'Duncan said." I know that, so why don't you tell me something I don't know, like when you people is going to find the son of a bitch, who broke into the shop, and set me free. We got the son of a bitch 'Duncan, reply gingerly.

Can I ask this question please? Do you wander why the other assholes beat the crap out of me? Well I will tell you, it's because all you son of a bitch's treats me like a wild animal.

I told you the hand cuff is two tight, and you took no notice, you treats me like I am a dam fool, like I don't know when I am hurting.

As long as you treat me like I am stupid, I will be as nasty as I can, because I don't care anymore, I don't care if you all gang up on me, and take turns beating the crap out of me, or kill me, I don't care a shit what you do.

I hope that answer some of your questions, I hope you find out treating me like an animal won't work; I will never answer any of your questions, until my lawyer is in the room.

I told you this, but you took no notice, so I will just sit here and listen to your questions.

Then 'Duncan, got up, I sit back up right waiting, as he came towards me.

I got up and drop to my knees on the floor, and roll myself unto my side, into a ball.

I thought if he is going to hit me, he will have to get down on the floor to do it, or kick me while I am down and helpless.

He stood over me for a while just looking, I could see his shinny black shoes; as I lay very still wandering when was he was going to kick me.

After a while he walk pass me and out the door.

A few moments later I could hear foot steps, walking down the passage, and enters the room.

"Come on get up he said.' I did not move.

Get up, let officer 'Dillon, fix the hand cuffs he said.

I got back on my knees, but I could not stand up.

Officer 'Dillon, help me up, and loosen the cuffs.

Take him in the next room 'Ned' please; "Ok" 'Mr. Nelson.

In the other room there was more distance between us, the room was bigger and the table was larger.

"Okay' we are all safe now, and none of us is hurting any more are we," a sneaky wise crack from "Nelson."

Like hell I am not safe, the both of you can kick the shit out of me, anytime you want.

I still have the hand cuff on.

"You can forget it, 'Duncan, said, we won't remove them."

Why do you all think I am guilty I ask? They did not answer; does nobody in here believe

I am innocence? I'll say it one more time I did not break into that blasted shop; the only thing I am guilty of is been a half breed as 'Gurney, call me. That's why he arrests me.

"Tell me how you work that out "Nelson asks?" Work what out I ask? 'The shop keeper said a black man broke in with machete,' and he said he saw you. 'Do you want us to believe they are lying?' Yes.

"Why should they lie?" Because the cleaver bastard, 'Gurney, came to the nearest house with black people, and arrests me. That's how I work it out.

"So what you are saying detective Gurney and 'Mr. Jenkins, is lying?' Yes.

Who the hell is Mr. Jenkins? "He is the shopkeeper."

Gurney, the cleaver sons of a bitch almost kill me; because I would not answer his questions without my lawyer present.

So please give me a good reason why I should answer your questions, without a lawyer present.

I did not trust "Bigfoot" so why should I trust you lot.

"Nelson said "Ok,' 'Ok,' contrary to what you think, we are not here to beat you up or trap you."

"We are here to hear your side of the story."

"Tell us what happen between you and detective;' before he could say his name again.

I said Bigfoot.

"Detective 'Gurney he said." You can call him what you want, I'll call him Bigfoot.

I will say it again I am willing to talk with my lawyer present; I would also like a copy of what Bigfoot said happens in that room.

"That's" all I have to say until my lawyer is present. They got up and walk out.

Maybe they remember that I stop speaking to them when I was in the hospital.

Even thought they keep asking questions, and threaten me with the law.
I sat there for at least half an hour.

And then another police officer came in, this time in uniform, he was very neat; he did not have a hair out of place.

He had a beautiful, shinny crown, and pips on his shoulders; medals ribbons fill his chest.

He slowly pulls the chair out sit down, opens a folder and look at me, but said nothing, then look back at the folder, and start reading; he did not tell me his name.

Rub his eyes, yarn, rub his eyes again.

"Let us see if we can straighten something's out," let us try and get to the bottom of it, so we can put it right."

The way he speaks, it was plain to see he was thought "English" in a private school.

It was impossible for him to put that accent on.

I thought that's cool, this one has a mouth full of marbles.

Let us do that I said mockingly posh,' where is my lawyer? 'He did not answer; we just look at each other for a while. Goodbye I said.

"Where are you going he asks?" Not me, you are going I said.

'Ha, ha, very funny he said, we have comedian here."

"Well Mr. Comedian I have news for you," we can do this the easy way, are the hard way."

"Which is it going to be?" Please may we do it the heard way first? But before you start, please tell me how many ribs you are going to break, and what side would you like to break them, left or right, so I can prepare myself. I could see he was getting angry, so I kept quiet,' and I totally ignore him. Then he said, 'I am Richard Renter, Superintendent Richard Renter to you." Sorry I did not introduce my self before.

"Well Jim I am here to hear your side, of what happen in that room."
It would be nice if you call me Mr. Sears and not Jim please.

Are you sure I ask? Am I sure of what he ask?" Are you sure you are here to hear my side of what happened. Yes I am sure he said.

Well for starter I am innocence, believe me or not. He starts to say something and stop, then pour some water in a plastic cup, took a sip, lit a cigarette, "want one he asks?" I look at him but did not answer. "Okay" he said I don't blame you, they are bad for your health."

Again he pauses for quite a while.

"Why don't you be a smart lad, and answer my questions." Look I told your friends, I will answer your questions with my lawyer present, until she is sitting beside me, you may as well go and fart in the wind.

He stares at me, and then he said.

"Contrary to what you think I am here to hear your side of this dreadful saga."

Is that what it is? My life is just a saga to you, well that's new; I did not know that, thanks for telling me."

"Hell now I know what I am doing wrong, thank you very much for telling me, I am having a saga, my life is a dreadful saga.

Please be kind and tell me how to put my saga right.

"You will talk, you will sing like a bird, by the time we are finish with you," I have seen some hard nut in my time," believe me we crack them all."

I sat there and look at him, and he at me,' I hear my belly rumble, and he herd it also.

"You are hungry good; soon you will be hungry, and sleepy."

It got dark in the room; he turns the light on, and arranges it so it shines in my eyes.

I close them; he got up and walks out the door.

A few minutes later the door open, I heard the chair pull from under the table again,

And new voice said I am.

I don't care a shit what you are, or who you are, I am going to tell you the same thing, I told the other fellow.

I want my lawyer present before I say anything.

What I said did not stop him saying detective 'Wyman. I kept my eyes shut.

But he still asks questions, to which I gave no answer.

Then he said "this is going to be fun; we are going to have a ball you and me."

"Are I am, I don't know about you," you are invited but, I don't think you will enjoy it."

Is that so I said, trying to see him, with the lights in my eyes, it was very bright.

So I close my eyes again and block him out.

Tomorrow is another day, ran through my mind,' she will be here tomorrow, I hope.

She said she would come back; maybe she won't, because I ask her to go to bed with me, surly she can't hold that against me, I don't think she is the type. I don't think she could blame a lad for trying.

As I drift back I heard him repeating some of the questions, and after a while he was just like an echo in the distance again as I slip away in my thoughts, because as far as I was concern; we were not in the same room, he was having a ball all by himself.

I focus all my thought on her; I was thinking of her that hard I could almost see her small black shoe under the table, and her slender long legs, her knee length black skirt, red jacket and white shirt. I could smell her "perfume" even thought she was not there.

He got up and pushes me, "wake up, there is no sleep for you."

I did not open my eyes, and I said that goes to show how stupid you are you can't tell when someone is a sleep or a wake.

He pushes me again; well to be honest I thought you died, he said.

When do I eat? "Did you say something he said?" So you can talk?" Well you face less, thing, whatever you are, do your worse, do whatever you want, you wont worry me.

I close my eyes again, and switch my thoughts back to 'Lisa, I imagine going to bed with her.

I was thinking about her so hard, I did not hear him leave the room.

How long have I been here I ask myself? I wonder am I loosing my memory, have they finally brainwash me.

Then I heard someone unlock the door, and pull me and the chair from under table and check the cuff.

My wrist was "swollen" I could no longer feel them; he took me back to my cell and remove the cuff.

"Here gave something to eat; he said."

I was so sleepy; food was the last thing on my mind.

When I put the first bit in my mouth it was cold, looking at the meat it was very fat.

So I drop the plate on the floor, spilling it.

As I fell asleep, they wake me up, and take me back to the same room for more questioning again.

They did this several times in night and the next day.

It was the same routine; so this made me even more determine to keep my mouth shut.

Sitting there wondering, when will 'Lisa come to see me, and then as if from afar she asks are you okay? At first I thought I was dreaming, so I answer just sleepy.

When I look up, I could see from her eyes, she knew what they were doing to me, but said nothing.

"You must answer there questions," if you answer there questions they will leave you alone."
I don't trust them, but I will answer their questions, if you are present.
She walks very slowly across the room knock on the door it opens.
Tell your supervisors; he will answer their questions now.
When she came back she sat down in the chair beside me.
The smell of her perfume was just like I remember it. That Perfume is nice I like it. Thank you she said.
I dream about you the other night I said, because that was the only thing I could think of to say. She, smile, "I bet it was good." Yea, it was good.
"So you did have a nightmare?" No. She was still smiling when the door open.
"You must tell me what it was all about sometime."
Are you sure you want to know? "Yes of course I want to know, she said very quiet."
With just a small nod and smile, as 'Duncan, sit at the table. He looks at us both for a while.

"Okay" let us get down to it "Nelson said, with a serious look on his face."
"But before we starts what is your full name?" It's 'Jim Sears.
"That was not so hard he commented, while writing it down."
"Miss Myrna this is what your client is charge with."
Breaking and entering, robbery, carrying a dangerous weapon, assaulting a police officer, refuses to answer questions, and insulting behavior."
May I ask why you don't go home and get your kitchen sink, also anything else you can find? Chuck it all in while you are at it,' round it off so it will look good on paper.
"Please excuse me gentlemen, while I speak to my client, "Lisa said."
She pulls me to one side of the room. 'Listen I'll only say this once.

She stood so close to me, I could feel her breath on my face,' I could smell her perfume close up for the first time, it took my breath away.
My heart was beating so fast, I almost had a heart attack. "Are you listening?" Yes I whisper. "Well only answer questions you are asked." 'Do not volunteer any information, and stop been "sarcastic," it wont help your case."
"Okay do you hear me?' Yes I heard you.

We went back to the table.

"Can we continue now detective 'Duncan asks."

She nodded, and in the same movement pick up her hair, and tuck it behind her ear.

They ask question after question, some they did not ask before, but others they ask several times in the previous questioning, "sessions."

I answer yes, no, and give no explanation. At one stage they just sat there and look at me.

They said nothing for so long; I thought they ran out of questions.

I could see by the look on Duncan's face,' he was not pleased with the answers; he was fidgety and wriggling in his chair and clinches his fist often.

You are not a happy camper I thought, you would like to hit me if you could.

'Nelson, on the other hand, was very calm, with very little expression on his face.

Now I was sure he is a real pro.

He did not twitch, or show any emotion, instead every now again he would stare at me,' with such intensity; it felt like his eyes was piercing my soul. Thank you 'Lisa, for been here, I thought glancing at her.

She sat very calm, playing with her pen between her long fingers.

Every now and again she would stop wriggling the pen, to look at her nails,' or jot something down,' but said nothing; I thought she is a real pro.

Suddenly they start asking a lot more questions; it was like their battery started working again. 'Then for the first time 'Lisa said don't answer that.' I yarn and shake my head.

'Duncan, was about to ask a question, when 'Lisa said. "Gentlemen, have you had enough."

Looking at there face, it was plain to see they did not want to give up.

My client needs a rest. "Rest" 'Duncan said he can rest later."

"You kept my client up all night, and a couple of days," looking at him. Who told you this 'Duncan, ask? 'Nobody I know the routine.'

'Duncan was not satisfied and he made it clear.' 'See you in court gentlemen she said, and stood up.'

They hesitate but got up and walk out.

She sat down again; "I think they will let you sleep tonight." Thank you I could do with a good night sleep.

"You'll be put in a line-up tomorrow," I won't be there, so just do what they ask," and you will be all right."

Why a line-up? "They could not put you in one before," because you were hurt, and 'Mrs. Jenkins, the shop keepers wife, she was very ill after that night."

See you in court, "she said and knock on the door."
The officer let her out, and he took me back to my cell.
Here we go again; the same routine, the hatch open and my food push in.
The hatch open again and a hand pick up the plate,' and I see part of a face looking at me.
Round and round the cell I walk, thinking of 'Lisa, with every step,' when I should be thinking of what is going to happen to me.
Next day I was taken to the line up,' the usual thing, turn right, turn left, face the front, stand there put this hat on, and we walk off.
Back to the cell I go, once again I walk around like a hamster on his wheel.
That afternoon I was hand cuff again, and taken to the interview room, and just like before they had more questions.

This time I answer every question, just like 'Lisa said, yes, no, and no more.
To my "surprise" they were reasonable pleasant.
Two days later I was given a letter from Lisa, asking for permission to get my clothes from my lodgings. I sign it. When I receive my clothes they were dry clean.
You will be going to court next week, the note that came with my clothes said.
Suddenly I was afraid, so, afraid my hands and knees start to shake,' that night sleeping was impossible.

They got me up early; tell me to get dress, treat me like I was a child. Fed me and hand cuff me.
Took me to a van, drove me to the court house, 'flank by two police officers.'
'Lisa, was there looking elegant as ever, she really looks the part.
'This is only a hearing, to decide if they should try you,' they will also decide if it is safe to let you out on bail.
'Judge Wilson, will set a date for the trial, if they decide to charge you.' So don't let it worry you yet she said."
When she finishes explaining everything, she asks how they were treating me.

Well I've had worse days. She stops talking as soon as 'Judge Wilson, walk in, and we stood up.

There was a lot of legal jargon, I did not understand. Then Judge Wilson said no to 'Lisa, several times.

I was so nervous I did not hear the question she asks.

Then he pauses, look at her intensively, he said, we do not think it's in the public's interest, to grant your client bail."

"Your honor my client, have never been in trouble before," his army records are "impeccable." "I" grant him this 'Miss Myrna, but his behavior now is disgusting."

"We cannot allow him get away with it; your client must realize he cannot do as he wishes. "Your honor she said again."

"Before she could say more," 'Judge Wilson said, 'Miss Myrna, my answer is still no."

I look at him, thinking the son of a bitch is going to lock me up."

And there is nothing I can do about it; he is going to do it now and later if he is the judge in charge when my trial comes up.

In his eyes I am guilty; he believes everything he's been told, 'Gurney cannot lie.'

I was that disgusted, sitting there; I had no control over what was happing to me.

When they set the trial date, I did not hear it,' I was so busy thinking, what the hell they are doing to me.

My heart was beating so fast and hard, I could hardly hear. 'Lisa, said something, but I took no notice.

The next thing I heard, as if from a far, was the officer saying come with me, and then 'Lisa said I'll see you tomorrow." "I'll explain it more in detail tomorrow."

"So don't give up, not yet, it's not the end."

In the station they remove the cuffs. "Pick up your stuff, one of the officers said."

They took me to another cell opens the door, said nothing so I walk in.

Sitting on the bottom bunk bed, was another prisoner, I look at him and he look at me.

"The top bunk is yours he said, can't stand been on top."

"I am afraid of heights; never get on top of anything not even a woman." Afraid I may fall off he said laughing." I took no notice.

"You are not very happy he said still laughing." This is going to be fun

27

I thought as he kept talking.

Don't you never stop I ask? "I talk a lot "don't" I? You are not kidding I said, hell I can't hear myself think, he took no notice.

"Is this your first time he asks?" It's very hard the first time; "by the way my name is 'Jerry, what's yours.' I did not answer.

"Man, you sure "don't" talk do you he said?" 'What did you do?" I still did not answer.

'Ha, well I better give my tongue a rest; he said reluctantly, and then said 'we'll talk later when you feel like talking." Thank you 'Lord, I said. He said what? I said thank you 'Lord.

'He said for what?' He made you shut up; the expression on his face was blank, it was as if I did not say anything.

"They will feed us soon; I hope they have something good he said,' I am hungry.

And then for a long time, he said nothing.

He just sat there for a minute and look at me.

After a while he lay on his back and look up under my bunk, as if there was something to see under there.

I could not believe he was silent; it was just like someone fond his switch and switches him off.

He was right the hatch open and they push the food in.

As we sat down to eat, he starts talking again. "You did not say what you did."

"What did you say I ask? 'Why are you, he stutters with his mouth full of food?"

His mouth was that full, he could "hardly" swallow until some fell from his mouth. "I said why you are in here?" "What did you do?" Nothing I said.

"Don't be silly they don't put you in here for doing nothing, he said."

That's where you are wrong; I am here for doing nothing. "You are the one that crack the detective nuts aren't you?" "You see you done something."

"The worse thing you can do is crack a detective's nuts."

Then he starts laughing, and almost chokes with the food in his mouth.

What is so funny I ask? "You cracking detective 'Gurney's nut, I should love to see his face."

"Believe me you could not have done it to a nicer person," and he kept laughing with the food falling from his mouth.

I had to laugh myself, because he was laughing so loud.

When he saw me laughing, it made him laughs even more, I though any moment he will have a fit.

"How did you manage to crack his nuts?" I did not answer, instead I ask, who told you about it? I heard the coppers talking yesterday when they took you out.

Who told you it was me? 'We pass you in the passage, you did not see me.

"Another time I saw you at a distance, they were taking you into the interrogation room."

"Two police women were talking about it and one point at you."

What did they say? "She said that's the prisoner who hit officer 'Gurney, that's all."

Did she say if he was alright? "Would you be alright with one of your balls crush?' Man I heard they had to remove it."

They remove it? "Yes he is a one nut case screw now he said, and he starts laughing again a lot louder than before."

When he stops laughing, I ask did they say what he and his partner did to me. "No." Only that you were in the hospital for a while."

So they did not say Gurney and his partner crack my skull and broke two of my ribs.

"No they only say you broke into a corner shop, with a machete in the night, and rob the shop keeper.'

So you heard I break into a shop? 'Yes that's what they say.' So why are you asking me what I did? "Just want to hear you say what you did." Why? 'You know why, they say one thing and you say another; "I want to hear it from the horse's mouth, that's all."

Well what they say is a lie. I did not do it, so here is my story, you can tell it as I say it.

I was woken up very early in the morning, by big foot detective 'Gurney and his side kick 'Bradford.

They took me down stairs half a sleep, and ask the stupid shop keeper if it was me, and the half dead son of a bitch said yes, that's him, and here I am, with two broken ribs and a crack skull.

"Who crack your skull?" Who the hell do you think? Do I have to spell it out for you? "Gurney, he said." I did not answer.

What did you do I ask? "He answered not a lot."

Have you been in here before, for doing not a lot then I ask? "This is my fourth time." You must be bloody mad. "No I am not mad, just not lucky."

How the hell do you work that out? "Work what out he ask?" You have so much bad luck, coming back here four times.

I "don't" know he said."

Well does that mean you will be coming in for a fifth time, I ask? I don't know yet,' but you take a tip from me," never carry a weapon when you go to do a job; it makes things worse for you."

'Jerry, I did not break into that shop, I just told you. "Pull the other leg he said."

Can you see what's wrong? If I can't, get you to believe me, how the hell am I going to get the law to believe me? Shit they are going to lock me up, and throw the blasted key away; this can't happen to me, this only happen to other people I shout.

For some unknown reason I did not trust this guy, he talks two much, he is like a time bomb waiting to go off, the only difference is he would not go bang. He would just repeat everything I say like a dam parrot, he was chatting away without a brain. I hope I "don't" talk in my sleep, or says something stupid. So he can tell the cops, that I say I done it.

Next day two officers open the door; I thought oh no not again. Come 'Jerry, he said.

He went out the door chatting to them like they were long lost friends. I thought when he is going to hug them,' and give them a kiss on the cheek.

Twenty minutes after they took 'Jerry, two officers came for me, put your hands on your head.' I put my hands on my head.' He put the hand cuffs on, and then gives me a push. Hold on I said there is no need to push me, I am not an animal.

"Well if you prefer, bloody move then he said." and the other said how would like me to kick the shit out of you instead?" Well my hands are tied, so help yourself, and if you can't do it by yourself get your buddy to help you. He gave me another push, "don't temp me he said." You don't have the guts, go on I dare you.

"I am going to tell you to move one more time." Good at least you tell me to move, you see there was no need to push me.

I move knowing he would hit me, somewhere where it would not show. 'Lisa was in the interview room waiting. "Hello Jim she said."

'Officer Will you remove the cuffs please."

"Are you sure madam?" Yes. He looks at her strange, and asks again are you sure you want to do that?" "Yes remove them please."

"How are you she asks again?" Will I've had better days? "How are they treating you?" Like an animal. 'Why?' I don't know why.

"Are you doing anything I should know about?" Like what? "Been nasty to them?" No.

It seems they can't forgive me, for what I done to big foot. "You could be right."

If they can't forget it; it is possible this will follow you everywhere you go, from now on.

'You look very disappointed when the judge did not give you bail.' Yes he found me guilty before the trial. 'I don't think so.' I do, you mark my words, he is going to put me down,' and he is going to make an example of me.

I'll be lucky if he don't string me up by my balls, sorry for the crude explanation.

'Lisa, he is going give me the maximum time he can give,' just for been in my bed, and there is nothing I can do about it.

Would you like to know what makes it so bad? I am innocence; the dam old man doesn't have enough in that shop, to give me a good night out.

This will ruin all my plans, I plan to study electrical engineering; I am taking a "correspondent" course.

I paid the entire course fee already; I was hoping to have a better job.

So I would not have to work so dam hard all my life.

This was going to be my way out; I would work my brain and not my body.

'Did you get any books from them?' Yes. "Are they in the room you rent?" Yes.

"I'll get them for you, if you give me permission."

Thank you, I think the police still have my keys.

You must keep up with your studies no matter what happen promise me.

I did not answer her; 'I want you to promise me this.' Okay I said. "Jim I mean it."

Okay I said again, I promise.

I could see from her eyes she was serious, why I did not know.

'Lisa, somewhere down the line, I know the truth will come out, and ill be free; I will need a lawyer when I sue them.

"Why are we talking about this, that won't happen for a while?" You have to get through the trial first.'

'So wait and see how things turn out, before you make other plans.'

When is the trial? I did not hear the judge? 'It will be two months from today.'

Thank you.

"Do you have any more questions she asks?" Yes but I can't ask them.

'Why?' She pauses, then said don't ask?" You may dream again, and that won't do you any good dreaming about me."

"If I were you, I would dream about how to get out of the mess you are in first, before dreaming about me, she said smiling.'

'Lisa, I have to find something, to take me away from the trouble I am in, and you are it.

"That's nice to know, that's all you want me for." I am sorry I did not mean it like that.

"Its all right I understand she said, smiling."

Believe me dreaming is good; because that's all I can do in here.

"Dreaming about me she said smiling again, you are crazy."

Why I ask? "Because I have to go now that's why." Well there go all my dreams again.

"You use that one before; you are a real charmer aren't you."

Who me? "Yes you," I can't see anyone else in the room can you? Bye, see you soon."

I'll be here, I have nowhere to go.

"Remember when you get those books; get stuck into them, they will give you something to do besides dreaming all day." When I return to the cell 'Jerry, was back, and right away his mouth start working over time.

"Did you have a nice day he asks, with that pretty lawyer of yours?" No I said.

"Hell it must hurt having a pretty women so close and you have to keep your hands in your pockets."

I've had enough of this shit house; I got to get out of here, before I go mad.

You can forget that; you do the crime you must do the time.

I snap, you "don't" fucking hear so good do you.

I'll say it one more time very slow, I did not break into that shop; I was in my bed when those assholes wake me. Do you understand me now? "Yes he said if you say so."

Well I hope you fucking hear me this time; because that is the last time I am going to tell you.

So if anyone asks you about me, remember to tell them I said I did not break into the shop. Can you remember that? "Who do you think will ask me about you?" I don't know maybe the police; they may get you to spy on me.

So if they ask you about me, tell them I say I did not do it.

He went quiet for the first time; with a guilty look on his face.

He had nothing to say for along time.

It was nice, because for the first time since I walk into the cell it was quiet.

I could almost hear myself think.

"Breaking the silence he said, we will have chicken tonight for dinner."

How do you know this I ask? "Today is Thursday; and we always have chicken on a Thursday." Jerry, do you ever have a shower? You need one now, right now, ask the screws to let you have one now please, this is a small room, and I have to live here.

Then I start to think they put me with him, as a punishment known his dirty habits.

He sat and look at me when I as him to have a shower, Jerry I am going to say it one more time ask them if you can go for a shower before I get mad.

I could not believe my eyes he did not care; his face was blank, like he did not hear me. Did you hear me? "Yea, 'yea, I hear you."

Then go and do it now before they bring the blasted chicken, so I can eat it without smelling you.

He got up slowly, looking at me with every step he took towards the door, he knock on it several times before it opens, and they let him out. When he came back he was clean.

'Jim, "if they lock you up with someone," who doesn't care a shit, and you tell them they stink as shit, you better watch it."

"There are some nasty people in side."

"There are people who will take no notice of you," but will cut your throat, while you're a sleep," so be careful who you tell to go and have a shower."

"You will have to learn to mind your own dam "business" inside, even if they are as stink as shit, you don't tell them."

"Jim, there is some real nasty people in prison."

Jerry, there is no need to tell me, I hate to tell you this; I don't care a shit either, so if anyone cut my throat, they better make a good job of it, because if I wake up it will be my turn to cut," so if "that's" what is on your mind please think carefully about it before you try.

Jerry, listen to me very careful here is my advice to you, do not don't try it, because I could wake up very mad, and believe me you wont like what I will do to you, and that's my last word on the subject, so don't ever forget it.

"Jim, I did not mean me, 'oh' no not me, I hate the site of blood." Good that's nice to know.

I could feel myself getting hot around the collar; he was looking at me, and for the first, with a sturdy gaze.

His face shows he was scared, his hands start to shake, and his lips tremble.

"Jim, I did not mean me he said again," with a trembling sound in his voice."

'No, sir that is not my style "oh" god no not me Jim," hell I try my best not offending anyone; you can tell me anytime that I smells.' I'll go and have a wash every time you say;" I don't want to offend you or anyone, no sir not me."

Okay 'Jerry, forget it, you said that before, so as long as you remember I won't take it lying down, you will be fine.

Just then the door opens. 'There is a parcel for you.' I did not move.

'Jerry took it. It is yours 'Jim.' Thank you, I took it and put it on the bed.

"Aren't you going to open it?" Later, just then the hatch opens. "Chicken he said, I was right, I love chicken," reckon ill marry one someday he said, and start laughing at his own joke.

Let me know when, I'll come to the honeymoon I said; and he started laughing so loud, I though he was going to have a fit. Man, I thought this is one stupid guy. After a long time he went quiet, then he said you know that could be fun, watching you watching me, on my honeymoon, doing a chicken.' And again he starts laughing.

I took no notice hoping he will give up, if he sees I don't care.

While I was eating, I open the parcel took the book out, and start reading.

"Books he said?" Yea just books I said, so leave them alone.

Better yet I'll show you them now so you won't have look at them later, when I am not here. It took me a few days to get use to reading, with all the distraction, around me.

'Jerry, was bad, but the thought of been in lock-up was worse.

I try very hard to ignore everything and everyone; but at times I could hear 'Jerry, asking questions, so I ignore him, and after a while he got use to me not giving him an answer.

I was very surprise one day when they came for me; your lawyer is her he said I did not expect her. So I said 'Lisa; "yes he said, and ask how many lawyer do you have." I did not answer. I was surprise he did not put the hand cuffs on, when he said come with me.

Hi 'Jim. 'Hi 'Lisa, we must stop meeting like this, I said joking.

'It won't do your reputation any good lock in a room with a bad man.
"You are in a good mood." I am glad to see you "that's" why. 'I don't think so she said with a smile.

Well let's put it this way, you are the prettiest woman I have seeing for weeks.

'Jim, there is one thing I can say about you," you are a charmer, and you don't know when to give up." No I am not, I only speak the truth. "You are still a charmer." Thanks I am glad you think so.

"Let's get down to it, are you ready for Monday?" What's happening Monday? 'You will be in court where have you been?" I found a way to escape in those books. 'Well, have you done any work; Yes. Do you want me to send it to the tutors?" Yes please. 'Well I'll send them in for you." That is nice of you, thanks for your help. "Don't mention."

"Have you had any visitors?" No.

For the first time she really looks at me, and I could see in it her eyes that she really wants to help me."

I'll wait out front, and pick up your work, and send it in. Thank you, I can't pay you. "That's no problem." Thanks a million.

"I'll arrange everything for Monday; all you have to do is be there, in good spirit."

"Is there anything else you can tell me about that night?" No. 'What did you do when you got home from work, did you watch TV?" No. 'So what did you do when you got in from work?" I cook my dinner and read that's all. "Did you go back out at anytime?" No. Did you go to the shop?" No I did not. "Jim it's alright I was only thinking if you went to the shop the old man may have seen you and forgot where he saw you.

"Okay' if I have to put you on the stand, remembers what I said," don't volunteer any answers," and only answer the questions you are ask."

"Don't" let the questions he asks; make you loose your temper."

"At times he will ask it one way, and then ask it again, phrasing it in a different way; it will be the same question, so listen to him carefully before you answer."

'Oh, the money they took from the house is mine; I save it out of my wages each week. They have no right taking it. "Did they ask you where you got it from?" No they assume I stole it. I don't think they had a search warrant to search my room either, If they did, they never show it to me.

"I'll check it out, don't worry they will return all your money."

'Lisa, I am going to be honest with you, I "don't" think they will let me go, they want my blood, and an easy case, and I am it.

They are going to put me down for cracking big foot nuts.

That is the reason why they will put me down,' breaking into the shop will take second place. "Don't think like that, you must think "positive" and you will win."

"Is there anything else you want to ask or tell me?" No. "Okay" then I'll see you Monday.

"Don't forget to give your work to the officer when you get back to the cell," I will mail them for you." "Tell the officer I am waiting out front for the papers, there is no need for you to wrap them I will do that."

She walks towards the door. 'Lisa, I said, she stop and turn a round, what is it this time?" Just want to see you smile. She smile and walk back to the table.

'Jim, "you know you have a big problem." Who me? 'Yes you, do you want to know what the problem with you is?" No, but please tell me. "You like to dream of something you can't have. 'Lisa, that is all I have in here, there is no harm dreaming is there? 'Well if it pleases you go a head dream as much as you want."

One, last question before you go can I take you out tonight? "Well I would love to see you do that, she said smiling." Thank you that was worth it, thank you.

"What's worth it she asks?" That smile I said, plus you did not say no to me taking you out. "Bye then, if that's all you wants." No I want more, but as you say.

"Bye, bye, see you Monday she said, cutting me short before I could say another word.

As I walk back to the cell with no hand cuff, and no insulting words, it felt very strange, I felt like some thing was missing from my life.

But as I walk through the door Jerry bought me back to reality, his first words were well did you have a good time with your lawyer.

"You have a nice looking lawyer." Man she is a cracker." Jerry how do you know this? I pause remembering my work.

Officer, please give this to my lawyer, she is waiting out front' thank you.

Monday morning I got dress very early, and they hand cuff me.

Two police officers took me to the court house.

As I sat down beside 'Lisa, I ask her for a piece of paper and a pencil.

She gave me a small note pad, I wrote I'll love you no matter what win or loose, fold it and gave it to her.

She wrote I am your lawyer you can't love me, go and love your nurse.

I wrote at the bottom, I don't have a nurse, and push it back.

She smile, and wrote, very funny, 'If you keep this up, I'll walk out on you, and you won't have a lawyer either." I wrote you won't.

"Why she wrote?" Just then 'Judge Wilson came in and we stood up; I thought just my luck.

I got the same son of a bitch who would not give me bail.

They call the shop owner first; 'Mr Jenkins, the prosecuting lawyer said to him, can you see the man who broke into your shop that night? "Yes sir he said, "that's" him."

Point him at him please.

He pointed at me.

I thought after all this time the son of a bitch still has it in for me.

Hell he must be loosing his marbles I whispered to my self.

I did not want to hear anymore, because I felt like getting up, and run out as fast as I could, and slap him a few times, to bring him to his senses.

'Lisa grabs my hand under the table. "Okay" she whisper, it's "Okay."

Mr Jenkins what were you doing when you first saw the accused the prosecuting lawyer asks? "I was in bed sleeping; he woke me and asks where the money is.

And what did you do? "I gave him all the money I had, when I saw the machete.

And what did he do? "He took it and asks if there is any more, I said that's all I had.

And what did you do? "I did nothing; we just lay there scared, wandering what he was going to do next.

You said we? "Yes sir, me and the wife."

So you had a good look at him? "Yes sir I did."

So you are quite sure this is the man you saw? "Yes sir I am sure."

The prosecuting lawyer said to 'Lisa, your witness. "Lisa did not ask him any question, but reserve the right to call him later. "Call 'Mrs. Jenkins, please."

The prosecuting lawyer asks her the same questions.

Seen her for the first time, she looked ill and very nervous, and unsure of what she was saying when she answer his questions. She was shaking and sweat was running down her face. So her lawyer assures her there is nothing to worry about. I thought any moment they will get the doctor, to her, and the trial will stop.

I was lost, almost in a dream like state, looking at Mrs Jenkins, when 'Lisa's, voice brought me back, I heard her ask did you see my client very clear.

'Yes, she answered, in a crisp clear voice."

"Mrs Jenkins was there a light on in your room," if so who put it on?" 'No the light was not on.'

Did you or your husband, or my client put on a light at anytime, while he was in the room?" No she said.

So there was no light on in the room, at anytime. I said there were no light on. "Mrs Jenkins was the curtains drawn?" Yes they were drawn.

So there was no light, and the curtains were drawn.

So will you please be kind and tell me and the court, if there was no light on in the room, and the curtains was drawn how did you manage to see my client with the curtains drawn? "The street light is very bright out side the window." The street light is bright? "Yes."

Did you say yes? Please speak up so everyone can hear you.

I ask were the curtains drawn. "Yes."

I still can't hear you Mrs Jenkins. "Did you say no?" "No I said yes."

Well how far away from your bed was my client standing when he was in your room? "What did you say, she asks?" I said how far away from your bed was my client standing, when you saw him for the first time?" She did not answer.

Come on Mrs 'Jenkins, if you could see him, surly you can estimate how far from your bed, he was standing.

Was he by the side of the bed, or at the bottom of the bed? "He was moving around all the time."

So he was moving around all the time he was in the room? "Yes." Well if he kept on the move, what your best estimate would be was he touching your bed or closer to the far wall as he was moved around.

Do you wear glasses 'Mrs. Jenkins? "Yes, but I can see quite well, with out them."

Did you put them on while he was in the room? "No."

How well is quite well Mrs Jenkins, six feet, or twelve feet? "My room is not twelve feet wide."

So your room is not twelve feet wide, how about eight feet? "It could be ten feet."

Well 'Mrs Jenkins, what you are saying is, without your glasses you could see my client ten feet away in the dark, with dark skin even thought he was moving around all the time? "Yes, I could see him very well."

Mrs Jenkins how old is you? "I am sixty-one."

Mrs Jenkins, will you please remove your glasses.

Can you see that lady down by the door? Please will you describe the colour of her dress? Please do it without your glasses. "What lady?" Mrs Jenkins there is only one lady by the door.

The more questions 'Lisa asks her, it was plain to see she was getting very nervous, and her answers were getting very quiet. 'Lisa, ask her several times to speak up please.

After that I did not hear anymore, 'I just sat there day after day, asking myself, why they are doing this to me.

How many more lies can they make up? Why I am here, most of the times I feel like making a dash for the door.

Then they bought out the money that detective 'Gurney, took from my suitcase, and he took the stand.

"Detective 'Gurney, is this the money you took from my client room?" 'Lisa asks, "Yes Madam, that's my signature on the package.

'Lisa, opens the packet and removes a few notes, and looks at the numbers, and matches them with the list of numbers she brought with her. I am sorry your honour, 'Lisa said."

This money belongs to my client. You'll find all the numbers on this list.

Your honour these notes were paid to my client, by the company he works for.

'He told me, he saves it from his wages.' I had these numbers from the bank that is responsible for the wages of his company.

'She gave the numbered list to another gentleman, and he took it to 'Judge Wilson.'

He pauses, took a quick look, and gave it to the Clark of the court to check. He went away to check them. When he came back, he hand the 'Judge Wilson, a piece of paper.

He looks at detective 'Gurney, all the money belongs to the defendant. He wrote something down, but said nothing.

I could see the gloomy look appear on 'Gurney's face, but he said nothing.

Then 'Lisa asks did you find anymore money in my client room? 'No.'

"I can't hear you detective; I ask did you say no?" 'Yes, I said no.'

"So if you did not find anymore money, what did you find?" Nothing he said.

"You fond nothing, so if you fond nothing would you be so kind," please tell me and the court if you didn't mind anything, why did you arrest my client?" 'Mr and Mrs Jenkins said he was the one in their bed room with the machete.

"Well detective did you find the machete?" No

"Still questioning 'Gurney, 'Lisa, ask, can you please describe to me, and the court how my client got two of his ribs broken, and crack his skull?"

He attacks me, and I had to defend myself; so I punch him in the gut. "You punch him in his gut?" 'Yes.'

"What you are saying is, he suddenly got up and attacks you?" 'Yes and that's when I hit him in the gut. "You hit him in the gut?" 'Yes.'

Then he hit me in my private, and I fell on the floor, and he got down on me.

"He got down on you?" Yes. And that's when, my partner detective 'Ronnie,' I mean detective 'Bradford, step in and drag him off me.

He was like a mad man. "So please explain to me how my client got his skull fractured? He hesitates.

Did you crack his skull after you got up or before? 'No, It happens when detectives 'Ronnie sorry detective 'Bradford, pulls him off me.' "Detective 'Bradford, pull him off you?" Yes. "I'll ask again detective how did my client cracked his skull."

It happens when detective Bradford pulls him off; he hit his head on the wall. "He hit his head on the wall?" 'Yes.' Will you be so kind please, tells us again, how my client head hit the wall?" I said it happen when detective Bradford pulls him off me. 'Detective Bradford pulls him off you. "So when did you break his ribs?" Did you break them then or when you got up?" No it happen when I hit him in the gut the first time.

"So what you are saying, you hit him in the gut and broke two of his ribs while defend yourself?" Yes, I broke his ribs defending myself.

"And with two broken ribs he still got down on you?" 'Yes, I told you he was like a mad man. "He was like mad man?" Yes that's what I said. "Are you a doctor detective?" No.

"So how do you know he is mad?" He acted like he was mad. "He acted like he was mad."

Would you like to know what I think really happen in that room detective?" I think the both of you beat up my client," I think he was only defending himself the best way he could." Is that the truth?" 'I object me Lord, the prosecutor said.' Sustain, 'Judge Wilson said.' "Lisa, apologize."

I thought you bastard Wilson, and twitch on my seat, but kept calm.

"You said he attack you?" Yes, that's what I said. Just how heavy would you say my client is detective?" He did not answer. "Come on, surely you can estimate that."

"How, about one hundred and fifty five pounds, would you say that is a fair estimate?" Yes.' I can't hear you detective, please speak up. I think a hundred and fifty pounds is a reasonable estimate. "So if you think he is a hundred and fifty five pounds is fair," tell me please, if you were one hundred and fifty pounds, would you attack two grown men twice your size in a small room?" Again he hesitates. Come on she said, I need an answer. He suddenly attacks me, so I defend my self.' That is not what I ask you detective. Would you like me to repeat the question? 'Yes.'

"I ask you if you were the same size as my client would you attack two men twice your size in a small room." No but he was mad at the time.

"I ask you before detective are you a doctor, you said no, so why do you persist in calling my client mad?" Because he acted me like was mad. "Does he look mad to you sitting here?" 'No, but he was a different person that day.

"He was a different person," 'Lisa, repeats. "So if I shout to you, telling you are hurting me, and tomorrow you see me would call me mad."

All I can say he was different that day, he was evil.

"That was not the question I ask detective."

"Do you expect me and the court to believe that?" Yes, the man is evil.

I don't think so; do you want to know what I think? I think you are a liar, and not a good one at that.

'I object,' 'I strongly object,' I object the prosecuting lawyer said again very loud." Sustain 'Judge Wilson said again.

'Again the bastard sustains. What is the matter with him? What the hell is going through his mind? It was plain as daylight he was going to put me down, no matter what 'Lisa did or say. She may as well pack her bags and go on a long holiday.

I apologize, your honour 'Lisa said; but these gentlemen make me feel sick, expecting me to believe a story like that, and worse of all the court.

I am finish with this thing who call himself a gentleman.

Again the prosecutor object and 'Lisa apologises.

I had a good look at her face, as she walks back to her seat. She was not pleased.

Do you have any more questions 'Miss Myrna?' 'No your honour,' but I will call 'Mr Jenkins, back to the stand please."

"Mr Jenkins, the night in question did you have a night cap," before you went to bed?" "He was startled by the question."

Then 'Lisa, said surly you can remember if you had a drink before you went to bed?" 'Yes I did, but I was not drunk. "You were not drunk."

"How many did you have, and what was it?" I had two drinks of whisky; it was just a little drop to relax me. I have some most night."

"You have some most nights." 'Yes.'

"Do you wear glasses 'Mr Jenkins?" Yes I do. "Can you see without them?" 'Yes.'

"Please tell the court how far away from your bed was my client standing when you saw him?" He was standing about six feet away. Did you or your wife put a light on in the room?" He said no. Mr Jenkins, were the curtains drawn; no the curtains were not drawn. "Lisa repeats the curtains were not drawn.' Yes I said they were not drawn.

And what time exactly would you say, you saw my client in your bed room? I saw him about twelve O'clock midnight, or just after, I did not look at the time.

And what time would you say, you had your little drop of whisky?" And how little was the little drop?" He hesitates.

"Come on surly you can remember that?" Was it nine o'clock, ten o'clock, or eleven o'clock? 'About ten o'clock.' "

Did you fall a sleep right away?" Yes I was tired.

So you were tired and half drunk, and half blind, yet you could remember the face of my client with dark skin in your room, that had no light?" Yes, it was him.

"Have you ever seen my client in your shop before Mr Jenkins?" I can't remember.

"What if I tell you, my client has been in your shop twice before, once you serve him, and the other time your wife serves him?" Would you believe that?" I don't know.

Mr Jenkins, I ask you again, do you believe my client been in your shop before.

I said I don't know,' but it's possible. But I still "don't" know if I seen him before.

"Mr Jenkins, can you see the street from your shop window? 'Yes.'

"So what if I tell you my client walk, pass your shop everyday morning and evening to and form work."

"And it is possible that's where you saw him?" I object your honour, 'Mr Jenkins, said the first time he saw the "defendant" he was in his bed room,' and he is quite sure that's where he saw him for the first time, and no where else. Your honour, the prosecutor said I object.

Objection sustains Judge 'Wilson, reply.

"Your honour I am sure 'Mr 'Jenkins, must have seen my client more than once.

'Miss Myrna, 'Mr Jenkins, said he never seen him before, and if he did he can't remember.

Your honour it is possible 'Mr Jenkins, saw him, and made a mistake, where he first saw him, because he was half drunk, and half a sleep.

I object your honour, the prosecutor said again, there is no proof 'Mr Jenkins, was drunk.' "I am sorry 'Lisa, said again."

I have no more questions, for this half drunken half a sleep, half blind gentleman.

I object your honour; there is no proof that 'Mr Jenkins was drunk, half a sleep, or half blind.

I apologize, your honour, 'Lisa said again, and sits down.

'Judge Wilson, look up at the time, we will continue tomorrow.'

This is it, tomorrow I may know if he is going put me down.

Deep down I am sure he will put me down.

Because no one saw me in bed that night, and worse of all, I crack a detective 'Gurney's, nut.'

Lisa, looks at me, sees you in the morning, then start putting the papers in her brief case. She pick up the little note pad I wrote on, look at it and put in her case.

Bye I'll see you tomorrow she said.

They put the cuffs on again, I am getting fed-up of this I turn round and look at the officer putting them on. 'I am sorry but I have to do it he said.

That was an unexpected answer; they always insult me before.

Maybe it is because Lisa was standing so close to me, why he did not insult me.

I said bye 'Lisa and we walk away.

When we got in the van, the same police officer said to me, 'you don't look the type to rob a shop, with a machete.

Man this is a nightmare; I did not break into the blasted shop. I said angrily, and I am sick and tired of been treated like an animal.

He did not say any more, nor did I, for quite a while.

Then he asks about big foot.

'Did you hit detective 'Gurney, in his nuts?' Yes.

I explain what happen to him, he listen but said nothing.

When I finish he said want a cigarette. I did not answer.

'Would you like a smoke?' No thanks I don't use them.

That's good because you can't get them in side that easy, he said.

Then I ask myself why is he been so nice to me.

Well it possible he wants to talk just to pass the time away.

Next day, bright and early they got me up; we sat in a little room waiting to go in the court room.

'Judge Wilson and the jury will decide my fate, the thought keep running through my mind. I have this feeling deep down; they are not going to let me go.

The officers stood up, 'time to go.' My knees start to shake as we walk in and sit down.

Hi 'Lisa. Morning 'Jim, are you alright? 'Yea I am fine; 'we stood up as 'Judge Wilson, walk in.

'Please call your witness 'Judge Wilson' said looking at 'Lisa.'

"Your honour I call my client 'Jim Sears."

"Jim, please take the stand. Then I was sworn in.

Do you swear to tell the truth and nothing but the truth,' I thought that is a laugh, because no one told the truth yet, and I am the only one have a reason to lie, and they are asking me to tell the truth.

"Mr 'Sears, may I call you 'Jim?" Yes please.

"Jim, you were arrested on the sixteenth of November," and taken to central police station?" Yes I was.

Can you describe to me and the court what happen in side the station?" Yes.

I was taken to a small room, by an officer name 'Don.

I don't know his last name, He asks me my name, and I said the hand cuff is thigh.

"Did he remove them?" Yes, then he ask me my name again, and I ask him what did I do? And why am I under arrest? He asks me my name again? And again I ask what I did.

He would not tell me, so I told him I want a lawyer.

Then he said I have had enough of your crap and leave the room.

"What happen next?" When he came back, detective 'Gurney came with him, he is the officer who took me to the station. The first thing he said as soon as walk through the door is what is your full name? And I ask him what I did. He said I broke into a shop.

I ask can I have a lawyer present before I answer any questions.

He spun me around in the chair, and say you are a clever son of a bitch aren't you?" And I answer yea.

And the next thing I knew me and the chair was on the floor, on the other side of the room.

"How did you get over there?" Detective 'Gurney, slung me and the chair across the room, and the chair tip over with me.

"What happen next?" I try to get up, when I was almost up; he punches me in my gut, with my back against the wall, I fell to the floor; in the hospital they told me I broke two ribs. "Who hit you Jim?" Detective Gurney hit me. "So what happen next?" He stood over me until I got on my knees; then I hit him as hard as I could in his balls, and when he fell on his knees, I hit him again this time in his gut.

"And what happen next?" As I was about to hit him a third time, detective 'Bradford, grab my arm and sling me across the room, this time my head hit the wall, and I felt blood gushing from my nose, and the next thing I remember is when woke up in hospital.

"Did you at anytime threaten detective 'Gurney, or detective 'Bradford?' No, I did not threaten them. Lisa turns and says your witness.

"Mr 'Sears, in the house where you were arrested did you threaten detective 'Gurney, on the stairs?' No.

"Did you whisper stupid pig, and fuck you?" No. 'You are lying.' No I am not.

"Well if you are not lying that means detective 'Gurney, is lying?" Yes he is, he calls me a half bread son of a bitch, walking up the stairs, when I stop and ask him what I did, he said because of me he lost a night sleep, so if I know what's good for me I must keep going. "Do you expect us to believe that?" I don't care what you believe, but that's the truth.

45

"So where you were the night the shop was robbed?" I was at home in bed.

I got home; I got home about five o'clock and stayed home.

"What did you watch on TV?" I don't have a TV. That's all your honour.

When he said "that's" all, I did not believe he finish.

I expect him to ask a lot more questions, and really put me through the grinder.

To make his case even stronger, but for some unknown reason he did not.

'Judge Wilson, looks at the clock,' and said we will have final argument tomorrow.'

See you tomorrow 'Lisa said, and start putting her papers together.

"May I have your final argument please?" I was hearing everything they say, but I could not believe what they were talking about me, they went on for so long, it seems like time stood still, as I sit there, listening to them.

The prosecuting lawyer kept on and on. I never heard so much crap in my life.

Does he really believe what he is saying I ask myself? The bastard is making it all up.

I whisper, and 'Lisa heard me. She gave me a gentle push. Then 'Lisa gave her final argument.

And the jury left the room; they took me back to the station to wait for the verdict, it, took them two days, before they came back, with the verdict, guilty on all charges. My hands and knees start shaking, when I heard them say guilty.

I look at 'Lisa, I could see she was shock, at the result, we'll 'appeal,' 'She said very quiet.' I look at detective 'Gurney's, face, the expression on it was clear to see, it was saying I got you, you son of a bitch.

I look at him I whisper fuck you one nut, you son of a bitch, I'll get you one day, and I hope he can read my lips, because no sound came from them. A few weeks later I was in court again.

'Judge Wilson looks at me eye ball to eye ball, without blinking, and start giving me a lecture, telling me what I can't do, and that society cannot accept my behaviour.

He rambles on so long; I thought why you don't shut your cake hole; you know you are going to put me down so why don't you get on with it.

Then he said six years, to the best of my knowledge. I did not want to hear all the crap he was saying, so I switch off, with disbelief thinking why is he saying and doing this to me; surely he does not believe he is right, if he does, the only thing I can think of, he's got shit for brain.

The son of a bitch is screwing me as hard as he can. I hope I have the chance to look you in your the eyes one day, the way you are looking at me now. When, he was through talking, I got up sir I have this to say to you, I did not break into that shop, but I did crack detective 'Gurney, nuts in self defence.

I would do it all over again and enjoy it, because "that" is, the only way I could stop him, beating the crap out of me.

Someday some how the truth will come out mark my words, and I hope you are around to see it.

I'll be back, this I guarantee, and I hope you are here to tell me you are sorry.

Quiet 'Judge Wilson shouts, hitting his desk over and over again shouting quiet, quiet.

'I'll say it for the last time, be quiet.' What the hell are you going to do if I don't shut up? You can't shoot me. I am innocence that's my last word, you remember I said it.

You better remember me, I shout. I'll be back; this is not the end, not by a long shot.

'Lisa was pulling my arm, all through my out burst, but I took no notice.

Then 'Judge Wilson, said to the officers take him out of my site.

The police officers grab me check the hand cuffs and start pulling me towards the door. "Jim, I am sorry she said." Remember the note I said. "Its, okay, don't worry about it she said." Lisa, it won't be long before they have to let me go, this I am sure of, so don't appeal.

I'll make them apologize, including that stupid Judge, if it is the last thing I do, I was shouting so he could hear me, but he took no notice.

That evening 'Lisa came to the station "Jim, I am sorry," I'll appeal." 'Lisa, it's my fault I did not think anyone would find me guilty, anyone in there right mind that is, and worse of all, for something I did not do.

The reason they found me guilty is because I crack 'Gurney's nut, the jury could not see pass that, they thought anyone who is capable of doing that to a cop, can also rob a shop.

What they could not see is I acted in self defence, when I hit 'Gurney.

'Jim, we will appeal, I'll put it in ASAP, don't give up, please stay focus, and don't do any thing stupid will you.

Well at least I know someone is on my side, thank you for trying.

All I can to do now is dream my life away for six years. "No "don't" do that, let's wait and see what they do when we appeal.

So I still have a chance I said smiling. "You know you are impossible, has anyone ever told you that?" Here you are facing six years in prison, and you are still joking.

I start to say Lisa. "Jim please stops now, don't say anymore."

Then she smile and say be a good boy please go before I say something I don't want to say.

That could be good I said. "No it could be bad," it would be unprofessional, and it could get me in trouble."

Well you better not say any more.

We shook hands see you soon I hope bye.

Wait for me I whisper, she did not answer or react, she just smiles her usual loving smile.

That night, I am sure it was the longest night of my life; I could swear the walls were closing in on me.

If it was not for 'Lisa, telling me not to give up, I don't think I could get through the night.

I ask myself several times in the night, am I clinging to an impossible dream?" After along time struggling with all the night monsters I fall a sleep.

It was a waste of time going to bed, because suddenly the cell door opens, and the light came on.

Standing in the door way, big foot looking very sure of him self.

"I am here to wish you, a safe journey, and may all your troubles be small ones, you son of a bitch, he said mockingly." Thank you, you are so kind I said, for been so kind may I ask how you are getting on with just one nut.

I bet you can't screw as well as you use to asshole.

I bet your wife is starving.

He starts to move towards me.

'Jerry got up, what time is it he asks? And big foot stop, and step back. "Well have a good time where you are going."

I know that place; you will have a lot of fun everyday, if I were you I would watch your ass.

Thank for your tip I will do that, but please don't say good bye yet, I know we will meet again soon. Have fun he said again. And you I said with your one nut.

"Oh" and please remember me the next time you try to have a screw, please tell your wife when you can't satisfy her that I am the one that cause you to screw to one side, and if she can wait six years I will be out, and in my prime.

Thank you I said again, missing nut, we will meet again I am sure, so take care.

I guarantee we will meet I said.

'Is that a threat?' Why should I threaten you, you can only beat inmates, when they are in a cell with no witness.

If you feel like loosing your last nut please let me know, I can arrange it.

His face went very red.

Then he said I better go before I get myself in trouble.

Yes I think that's a darn good idea, you better go and enjoy your one nut while you can.

Before he closes the door, I took a long look at his face, It was as red as a beetroot; I thought any moment he it was going to have a heart attack, because it was plain to see he was not a happy camper.

My broken ribs were getting better each day, but sometimes I get very bad headaches; I was worried about it, until the doctors told me that will go in time.

Again the door open are you ready, I was still getting dress.

"Hurry up the officer said, you still have to eat breakfast so hurry."

I had a quick drink off coffee, and he took me back to the cell to collect my stuff.

When I step out side on my way to the van, it was raining and very hard, it was very cold.

You would not believe it, even the weather is sad to see me go I said. "We are not," we are glad to see you go; no body here will miss you, one of the officers said."

Thank you, that is nice to know, now I can leave feeling very happy, knowing there is one place I am not welcome.

May I say this is not the end? You will remember me; you will hear about me again, you may even read about me that I promise you.

It was a long drive, so I ask where we are going.

"Why, are you in a hurry he asks?' No.

"So why do you want to know?" Asshole I whisper to myself.

"What did what you say?" I did not answer.

49

Again he asks, what did you say?" I look him in his eyes.

I said asshole.

"I hope you don't mean me." Why I ask?

He did not answer; so I ask do you think you are one, and then sit there waiting for him to hit me.

Instead he scratches his head, and looks at his fingers nails, and then stares at me intensely, if looks could kill I whispered loud enough for him to hear.

It's no wonder you are in trouble; you can't keep your mouth shut can you.

The beauty is someone where you are going someone will shut it for me; I don't have to get myself in trouble."

I ignore him and start reading my book. Every now and then he looks at the book, I could see he wanted to ask me some questions, but he did not

Suddenly the van made a sharp turn to the right and stops, then move a few more yards and stop again.

"You are home he said." "Enjoy yourself."

The door open we got out, and walk thought some very large iron gates. Hell gates I mumbled. "What did you say he asks?" I said you have good ears. "That's not what you say." So if you heard me why are you asking? "I would hate to be a round you for long."

Why I ask? "Because I would kick, the shit out of you that is why." Only if I lay down with the cuffs on, I reply.

I was unsure for the first time in my life.

At twenty-one this should not happen to anyone, what do I do now; I stop walking and look back to see the gates close, it was like an echo in my ear. "Move a voice said."

I did not move.

A hand pushing me in my back, bought me back, to reality.

The smell, and sound all around me heighten my senses, to such a stage I feel like running, but there was no where to run to.

I "suddenly" I start to shake, as I look from left to right. Seeing the inside of a prison for the first time, the feeling I am trap just like a rat.

'Hello 'Patrick, this is 'Jim, the asshole, he said to the guy on the other side of the desk, and right away 'Patrick, start to ask a lot of questions.

I totally ignore him and look away at nothing. "I am talking to you he said." I am sorry I did not know you could talk to assholes, I reply.

Then turn and face him, when I finally heard enough of his questions, I said why you don't shoot me, now I am here, I would be better off dead.

"Do you mean me?" Yes I mean you.

"Just answer the questions he said; don't give me any of your crap," I don't need to hear it; you are here for six years so deal with it." That's what you think.

"Just answer the questions, you cleaver bastard, can you understand Me." Just answer the fucking questions."

What the hell are you going to do if I don't? He said nothing; for a while, he just sat there with his hand on his chin and stares at me.

As if to say what I do next.

Then I said do you want to know something; you are so nice, do you know that?

I have never seen you before, and what do you do? You start rubbing me up the wrong way.

Do you know the best thing your mother could have done for the world? She should throw you out with the bath water.

"You would miss me wouldn't you, he said angrily?" Yes you got it right I said, the piece of shit and the piss that was in the water.

By this time I could see he was very angry.

Once again I was in trouble before the day began.

He was getting ready to hit me, and this time I know I ask for it.

What is wrong with me? What have they done to me? I am not the person I was five months ago.

Five months ago I would not hurt a fly, now I am angry with the whole world, what are they doing to me? When I finish answering some of his questions, in my brain, I ask did I piss you off. He said keep up that shit, and someone in here will fuck you up that's for sure." Man, believe me you will be lucky to walk out of here alive, and if for some strange reason you are lucky to walk out, you will be fuck up so bad, you won't know if it is night or day."

'Ha, well they better make a good job of fucking me up, as you call it.

He gave me my bedding, and tells me a lot of things, what I can do and what I can't do.

They took more photos of me, with a board with numbers I held up to my chest. 'This is your number he said, remember it.'

Once again I felt like I was in the army getting another new to remember, so I took no notice. I just did not want to know anything good or bad.

So once again I found that magic switch, and switch myself off.

Everyone I come in contact with seems hell bent in rubbing me up the wrong way, are beating the crap out of me.

So when I finally reach the cell I was in no mood to take anymore crap from anyone.

The guard opens the cell door and I walk in, the inmate who was sitting on his bed, his first words were, let's put you right from day one.

'He pointed, that is mine, that is mine, and that is mine, don't touch any of it,' I don't like people touching my shit.'

So I calmly say where my space is? He said there, and there.

So fifty percent of this cell belongs to me for the next six years? 'Yes he said.'

Well you listen, and listen real well.

Whatever you have in my space move it now, and keep it to fuck out of my way, as long as I am here, if you do that we won't have any problem "okay".

He did not answer. Did you hear me? He sat their looking at me.

So I put my stuff on the empty bed, and step back and look at him.

I thought here we go this is going to be good.

This is where one of us will be going to the hospital, but he just sat there and looks back at me. Did you here me I said again? Man this is going to be fun, I mumble, loud enough for him to hear me.

Okay we can do this the hard way, or the easy way, the choice is yours,' so what is it going to be? "Ok" he said I heard you and he move all his stuff, then sit down on his bed again and watch me.

Do you still have a problem I ask? 'No he said.' So why are you watching me? "I was just thinking he said it looks like we will be together for a long time," so we better learn how to get on."

"My name is 'Ron."

Hi 'Ron, mine is 'Jim. "Jim, how long, did I hear you say six years?" Yes six years.

"What did you do?" I did nothing. "They "don't" give you six years for doing nothing."

"That's" what I said, I did nothing.

"Judge Wilson, the son of a bitch, did not see through detective 'Gurney's and "detective" 'Bradford lies.

I pause took a deep breath. "You are right he said."

"Judge Wilson is a real asshole,' he doesn't care a shit if you are innocence or not."

"I heard people talk about him."

52

"Gurney and his side kick 'Bradford, beat the crap out of me, six weeks ago, before they send me here." What did you say I ask? "I said detective 'Gurney' and 'Bradford, beat the crap out of me." They beat the crap out of me also, about five months ago I said.

The bastards put me in hospital, but he did not get away with it.

I start to tell my story, and I stop. "They did not; get away with what 'Ron, ask?" 'What did you do to him?" Nothing I said.

I did not want him to know that I crack big foot's nuts, just in case he is like 'Jerry, and spread it all over the prison.

At least not from me, let some one else have the pleasure telling him.

But I'll remember him telling me about 'Gurney, beating him, when I go back to court, this could help me.

If I can find more people who big foot assault; if I can get them to tell their story in the courts this could help me.

I was like a drowning man grabbing at straws.

'Time to eat 'Ron said, and we walk down the stairs, to the dinning room; 'this is hell I thought.

As I follow 'Ron, to learn the routine from him.

Looking around at the men my heart skips a beat, thinking this is me for no reason. How can I take this for six years? 'Jim, we will sit here.' The sound of his voice bought me back, I was glad when he calls my name, because I was getting ready to scream, or do something stupid.

There was so much chatting between the prisoners, it sound like everyone was talking at the same time.

I could not hear what they were all talking about; it was just this continuous humming sound, just like bees caught in a bottle. After we ate, 'Ron took me for a tour.

I'll be honest I can not see why people commit crimes, serve there time, go away and commit another crime. .

Worse of all, the stupid fools come back several times, like 'Jerry.

There must be something mentally wrong with them, I said out loud.

"What are you talking about Ron ask?" "Don't" let it worry you I said I was thinking out loud I said.

I get like that sometimes, I lie to him.

Looking at some of the inmates faces, my thoughts start to wonder again.

It was plain to see they like taking things that doesn't belong to them; working for a living is hard.

Or maybe they are real hard cases, or think they are.

53

I'll be "honest" the only reason why I am not pulling my hair out, is because I know deep down inside, I won't be staying here for long, at least not for six years.

There is a good chance the son of a bitch who broke into that shop will do it again soon.

With that thought in mind, I can look forward to getting out early.

Looking at 'Ron, for the first time, he is over weight, have a big nose, his eyes was far apart, and his ears are big.

But when he speaks, I could tell he was no fool, Mammy and daddy must have sent him to private school. What the hell are you doing here I thought to myself but said nothing.

It was plain to see, he was a softy pretending to be hard, he is trying to fit in with the surroundings.

But as soon as anyone forces him into a corner he starts to look for a way out.

'Ha, 'Ron, what did you do to get in here I ask? I could not resist the thought of not knowing.

"I been clever he said." In what way I ask? "I con women," man if they want to give me their money, why should I refuse it."

"The one that put me here, I got eight thousands bucks from her." 'Hell man she was good to me in every way," but she had one problem I could not keep up with her."

Keep up in what way I ask? "Man as soon as you look at her she wants to go to bed."

What "don't" you like sex? "Yes I love it, but not when I am force to have it." Ron, no body can force you to have sex. "That's what you think."

You tell me how? "How about this, it happen just before I came in here, we decide to go out to eat," we got dress, and start to leave the house, when we reach the door step outside she stops, look at me come she said, we must go back." "Why I ask?" I want to she said.

"You want to what I ask," she did not answer.

"You want to what I ask again?" Let's go back into the house she said and I'll tell you. By the time we reach the sitting room, she had all her clothes off and half of mine.

"Man you would not believe, we done it just minutes before we got dress to go out."

'Ron, you mean you could not say no? "Man she did not give me time

54

to say anything." So how did she get it up? "Hell she shows me the pussy, and it came up." Well you could pretend.

'Jim, I don't know how to pretend, because once I am up I am ready to work."

"You want to know what makes it bad, when it stand up; it hurts from the top of my prick right down into my balls."

'Ron, I am sorry I can't help you I have never had that problem.

"Jim, believe it or not that's when I decide I must run for my life."

"When, you no longer enjoy sex that's the time to move on."

You don't enjoy sex anymore, I ask again? "Yes he said, the problem is, I was doing it for the sake of doing it."

"Hell we do it, we fall a sleep for ten minutes it seems, and she wake me wanting more." "Man I did not enjoy having sex that often."

'Ron, are you sure you are doing it the right way? "Jim, no matter what way you do it with this bird, you would still have a big problem," she just keeps coming back for more."

Maybe your tool is not big enough.

'Tool, man she needs a big sledge hammer hitting her on the head while you are doing it, and even then, the first thing she would say, when she opens her eyes is can I have it again."

I laugh out loud, and he went quiet for a while. Then he said.

"I been in here six weeks now; I could do with a bit of it right now."

"Funny how life is, when you have it you don't want it, and when you don't have it you want it."

'Ron, there is a saying where I come from. What's that he asks?' It goes like this.

Havie, Havie don't want it, "and Wantie Wantie can't get it.

That's true he said with a smile. We sat there for a while, saying nothing.

So I ask my self why do some men always try to make there sex life seems so much better, than it is, when they talk about it.

He made it sound so exciting; 'it makes me feel like I never had sex.'

Well it's nice to dream, so let him dream, it won't do him any harm.

Then he got up, "I'll give her a ring, and tell her how much I miss her," I'll beg her for some; she must be really hungry now."

"She must want it more than I do knowing her." Ron, she will kill you if you go back.

"Man that must be a nice way to die," can you imagine the headlines? Man murdered him self having two much sex."

55

"Screwing the doctors said he died with a smile on his face."
Very funny I said money and sex that's all you think about.

'Jim, I'll tell you this; if God made anything better he kept it for himself, "that's" for sure.
Ron, a few minutes ago you said you did not enjoy sex, now you want to die having it. "Jim, right now I could die for it, now I have had a rest."
"See you later, I must call her."
"When he came back he starts to explain to me what happen between him and her."
"You know the eight thousand bucks I took from her, it did not put a dent in her bank account; she has that much money," she will never live long "enough" to spend it."
Where did she get it? "Daddy and mammy left her a fortune," she is the only child."

Wish I could find someone like that, I would be so nice to her if she sneeze, I would cry.
For a fleeting moment, I remember 'Lisa and I think to myself, she doesn't have money.
She is a working girl.
What would she want with me, I have nothing and worse of all, I am branded a jail bird.
I am sure she would not touch me with a barge pole.
I can forget her and her money if she has any.
Again Ron was very quiet; then he said a man got to do what a man got to do.
He did not give me time to ask him, what he had to do.

Before he said, would you like to know what I wish right now?" What I ask? 'I wish I could grow another four inches on my prick, and another three inches in size." I would walk into that house with it." Man that could be a big surprise I said.
"Man he said I could really tickle her with it."
"You want to know something else; as soon as I get out of here I am going back to her," even it she kills me with it." Ron, I don't think she will kill you.

"If she is still mad at you, she will give you a good night and put you right back in here,"
If you treat her the same as you did when you were living with her.

56

It won't take her long to see through you.

It was as if I said nothing, he carries on saying what he was going to do to her, 'Jim, 'I am going to enjoy her money and her body."

"I am going to tell her how sorry I am, and beg her to forgive me."

"I am going to ride her ass night and day, until she begs me for a rest."

"I am going to let her feel like me wash out, and when she fall a sleep, I'll wake her up and beg her for more just like she done to me."

"I am not going to ask her for her money, she will be glad giving me it, to keep me happy."

What about love I ask? 'Love what's that?' If you don't know I can't tell you sorry.

He kept rambling on, as if she was the one that took his money.

Then I said, 'Ron, you did not hear a word I said did you.

The only thing you think of is money and sex.

"Jim, you got it right."

Well do you want to know something I said? "What he said?" I am sorry for her, having somebody like you with no feeling, life is short enough she doesn't need you, man she is a rich woman, she don't need you, she can get sex from any man.

Yours is not special, so the only thing I can think of is she loves you.

He looks at me surprise but said nothing.

Looking at him again, I thought to my self, she must be either blind, or bloody stupid.

Or the son of a bitch, have something only a woman can see.

Then I ask myself what the hell, does he take me for; he must think I am a fool to believe a story like that.

He suddenly got up, I am going to use the phone he said again and walks away in a hurry.

I sat there for a long time looking at nothing but the wall and the dark grey sky. This made me very depress, so I went back to my cell and start to read my books.

This is the first time I try to read in here, I found it very hard to block out the feeling of hopelessness and the noise did not help.

I will have to find a quiet corner somewhere, or find a way to block out the noise somehow.

So I put the book down and lie on my back and look at the ceiling, thinking how old is this place, when was it built, and how many prisoners done the same thing I am doing now since they built it.

After a while looking around the cell, I pick up my book again, and read a few more lines.

I was still finding it hard concentrate, so I went for a walk; I found the showers and some toilets, in more less an isolated corner, I walk in and have a quick look, there were three inmates walking out as I walk in.

I notice all three had there arms heavily "tattooed" also the bigger one of the three had a small cross tattoo in between his eye brows in blue and red.

They all look at me, said something to each other, and start laughing.

I took no notice.

Leaving there I walk for a while and then return to my cell.

Ron was back, and going through his things in a hurry as if his life depends on what he was looking for.

"Here he said, have a look here is my money bags."

Taking the photos from him, thinking she was an old woman looking like last night supper left on the dining table, with all the edges curl up.

I could not believe what I was looking at.

Man she is a dish, that's the only thing I could find to say; she is a dish, I repeat.

Looking like that and have money, it's got to be good.

How did you meet her? "I met her in a store," he said. How I ask?

We went to the same infant school for a while, and then she went to an all girl school.

When my parents sent me to an all boy school, I never saw her again, until I saw her in the store."

"She was buying something in the store," I found out later she owns it. I said to her I "don't" like that, but I fancy you."

That was corny I though, but I ask what did she say? Well I like it she said.

Still was looking down; so I ask are you buying it for your grandmother?" None of your business she reply.

So I ask her to have dinner with me, please don't say no.' she said no, still looking down."

"I was trying to see her face,' why I ask? I "don't" go out with strangers, especially cheeky strangers she said."

"If you have dinner with me we won't be strangers will we?" Then I said please let me die happy, have dinner with me."

"Have dinner with me please, my name is 'Ron, and yours is I ask?" 'Dee, that's a nice name I said.'

"I use to know a girl name 'Dee, in the infant school I went to, years ago, I said."

"Now we know each other very well, you know my name I know yours, will you have dinner with me?" She said "Okay."

"Thank you I said, and where would you like to go?" Will you choose the place and time? How about right now? And then she looks up at me. Dee, is that you? I was amaze, to see her.

Did you know it was me? "Yes she said that's why I did not look up."

It must be over sixteen years I said, since you leave the infant school. "Yes she said, fifteen years to be exact." You sure have grown, pretty than ever. "Thank you she said."

Are you married yet she asks? No, I have been waiting for you. You liar she said.

We walk out of the store, and have dinner, and a long chat, and from then on, she gave me everything I wanted.

"Man I did not have to ask her for anything."

I sat there looking at him and then the photos of her; I could see in his eyes that he was enjoying telling me his story.

He was enjoying it so much, he took the photos from me several times, and hand them back, without thinking of what he was doing.

'Ron, I said you are a fool she is a cracker, if I were you I would run back to her as fast as I could.

If the only reason you leave her is because she loves two much sex, surly you can find ways to satisfy her.

"Jim, she put me in here." Ron I don't blame her.

But if I were you, man I would creep back on all fours, she is a once in a life time woman, you don't find a woman looking like that everyday, and have money.

What did she say when you phone her? "She did not have a lot to say."

What she did not hang up on you? "No," she listens to me but did not hang up, until I say my time is up, I must to go." So I ask her if I could call her again she said yes."

He looks up at me, and walks out of the cell very fast.

When he came back he said I rang her again.

Why I ask? "I just had to ask her if she was still mad at me."

"She was quit nice, told me I was crazy, to do what I did, and I told her I was very sorry."

"I ask her if she could forgive me, she said she would think about it."

"I ask her if she would ring when she made up her mind, she said yes."

"So I beg her not to make me wait two long."

That's cool I said, at least she did not slam the phone down on you.

As they lock us in for the night, I felt so alone and hopeless, I have nothing waiting for me outside, no family not even a girl friend nothing.

I was feeling very sorry for myself; in the dark everything was larger than life.

It was a long time before I fall a sleep. I woke very piss off with life.

I took a drink of water, and was fine after I ate breakfast.

We took another walk, and Ron kept on talking about Dee," I almost ask him to shut up.

After a few days, 'Ron and I, was getting on like we knew each others for years.

We went into the exercise yard most days, and walk around for a while.

It was nice to go outside after been lock up in a cell, even though the only thing I could see is the walls and the grey sky.

This was still a shock to the system, knowing I was in a cage.

Before they kept me lock up in a building, now the building have an out side, with no where to go.

Ron was speaking to me, but I was so far in thought most of the time I did not hear him, and he did not repeat what he was saying so I let it go.

"Can we sit down now he asks?" No let's walk around a bit longer, we made one more lap and then sit, and watch the other inmates doing there thing.

This is it; this is what it's going to be like day after day for six years, gone through my mind, and my heart skips a beat, thinking that far a head.

Then I remember I did not break into the shop.

Every now and again there was scuffling among the other inmates, so this distract my thoughts, it took me away from my lonely thoughts and fears of tomorrow.

Some of the rows were very short, but some got very serious, at times I thought they would rip each other heads off, but them they always seams to stop short of doing it.

"Jim, in here, you learn to mind your own business, first rule look after number one. "Second rule look and "don't" see, third hear and "don't" speak." That sounds good to me.

When we went back to the cell, I got a letter from 'Lisa, my heart skips a beat, it was already open.

Do they always open your letters I asks? "Yes nothing is private in here."

I took it, fold it and put it in my pocket.

Ron, look at me, "are you going to read it he asks?" Later I said. "It could be important he said." So I took it from pocket and smell it, I could smell her perfume, it's from my lawyer.

"So you know her by smell he said?" Yes I do.

"You have a lady lawyer?" Yes. "Is she pretty?" Yea, then go for it he said.

What would a lawyer want with a jail bird? You would be surprise.

Go for it man, she is a woman and you are a man if you don't try you will never know, will you."

Will you leave me to read my letter, she put an appeal in for me, and she sends my work to my tutors, and she wants to know if I am still studying.

She said when she get the result she would. I pause; she would what he asks? She would send them.

All the best she said.

I will try and visit you as soon as I can.

That gave me some hope, knowing that someone outside of these walls care a little.

The days went into weeks, the weeks went into months.

But I did not let my work rate drop; even though I was piss-off most of the time.

I was determining to be an electrician when I got out.

Since I am going to be in here for six years, I will not the waste the time.

Lisa kept her word, she sent my work in on time, and sends me the result as soon as she got them, and she always sends a little note of encouragement in side, and ask if I dream of her lately jokingly.

She never forgot me saying, that I dreamt about her, but at no time did she give me a reason to think that she was interested in me, instead she pushes me to get on with my studies.

Ever now and again I would write I still dream. The reply would come back there is no harm in dreaming.

She never says any more, nor did I.

Then one day I was told to report out front, they took me to a room sit the guard said.

I start to sit in the nearest chair to the door, "no he said over there, where I can see you."

I went to the other side of the table and sit down.

The door open and 'Lisa, walk in, with a big smile.

That's nice I said. "What she asks?" Your smile I said, and ask if she had something nice to tell me.

61

She looks at the guard please close the door when you leave thank you, and remove the cuffs also please."

How are you she asks are you still dreaming? Yes I said.

"Good it may come true; she said it with a smile."

"Your work is brilliant she said."

"I told you I would come to see you, sorry I couldn't come earlier," I have a lot of work, but I never forget you."

Thank you at least there is someone out there who is helping me.

There is something I would like to say, I look deep into her eyes, thanks I said, for your help.

Is that all she ask.

No but "it's" the wrong time and the wrong place, I answered.

I thought I could see a slight hint of "disappointment" in her eyes, as she looks at her fingers. Then she said you could be right.

She reaches into her briefcase pull out some papers, "will you sign these here, here and here please?" I did.

"Don't you want to know what you sign she asks?" I don't have anything to loose.

The only money I have is the three hundred pounds, the police are holding.

Then she pulls out more papers, with out telling me what I sign, "this is your new work, and this is the result of your work."

Look at the result; you are good you should have gone to collage.

Once again her eyes beam with happiness, it was plain to see she was genuine.

'Lisa, you won't believe this, the inmate I share the cell with his name 'Ron, he was beaten by detective 'Gurney, and 'Bradford, about five months ago, when they arrested him.

I told him 'Gurney beat me, but I did not tell him the full story, good she said.

I'll try and find others; do you think it will help? "Yes, but be careful."

"You're in a place where there are no boundaries, some will tell you anything, and then tell the guards," something completely different about you."

"Others will lie, and use it to there advantage if they can, so be careful.

"We should hear from the review board soon so be careful."

What review board? "Sorry 'Jim, I did not tell you, I put your case back into the review board."

Then she looks at her watch, "I would love to spend more time with you, she pauses and look away, and back at me. "It's all work and no play for me, these days."

I know, thank you for coming I said, thank you for the smell of the perfume on your letters.

It reminds me that I must keep my sanity that I must still dream of heaven.

As I said it, her cheeks went red; she was blushing like a little girl.

"Goodbye dreamer she said shaking hand, I'll write you soon."

Do that please that's something to look forward to.

Bye I said and thank you again for your help.

She knocks on the door and we shook hands again, before they open it.

She walks in the door way and looks back before she went through.

I wink, and she smile.

I went back to the sit down as I sat there in a trance; severing the last whiff of her perfume the guard said you can go, still standing by the door waiting for me to leave, you know where your cell is don't you he said "Insultingly."

There was slight smell of perfume still on the papers she gave me.

When I walk into the cell 'Ron asks if I had a good time, did she bring you those books. Yes, yes to both questions.

"She must love you, does she have money?" I don't know.

"You're slow, if that was me, I would have some money already,' and know where she lives,' and I would ask her if she have a boy friend."

"Man I would know nearly everything about her in one hour, and have her in bed in an hour and half."

Ron that is why you are in here, I "don't" believe that, I don't believe any woman is that stupid I said.

"Jim, I been a conman all my life," I know women; and I know what they like to hear, and I tell them."

I did not say any more for a while, trying not to "encourage" him, instead I half listen to him rattling on.

'Ron, hold on I said after a while, she is my Lawyer, nothing else.

"Ha, he said, you would like more don't you?" I didn't answer.

"Come on, he said, yes or no?" No I said. 'You lie.'

'Ron, we are getting no where with this discussion.

"Jim, I am going to teach you a few things about women before we leave here."

Thank you I look forward to learn from the master.

Let's eat, let's go and enjoy the delights they have for us today, that may take your mind off women, and money, I said.

"That's impossible and you know it he said."

'Ron, you're impossible.

Out side the cell he suddenly stops walking, I thought he left something in the cell.

"Then he said, man you know I am a dam fool, I find one woman with everything," money, looks and a big brain that works a little two good," and what do I do?" I took her bread and spend it on others."

"Come to think of it, that is the reason why I could not keep up with 'Dee."

"That's" the first time he said the reason why he could not keep up with 'Dee.

"You know what I mean the amount of sex she wanted." He kept talking.

"Man I was screwing everything I got hold of." I thought here we go again bragging about his conquest.

"If I was giving it all to her, she would be "shagged" out, just like me. That's for sure she would be tired, because I was at it everyday.

"I was stupid; now I know I am stupid," I took her money and spend it on other women, just for a lousy few second jump," and once I get a jump I move on."

"Jim, I am a bloody fool," I was born with no brain, that's for sure."

"Ron its time to get down on your hands and knees and creep boy, beg you dirty dog, beg now for something you had and lost."

Is this the first time you been put down for ripping off women I ask? 'Yea, I had some close shave but got away." "You know 'Jim, its nice talking to you." Why I ask? "Because, you know where you are going; yea I am for dinner.

"No lets be serious, all I done with my life so far, is try to get into women's knickers as often as possible," and take as much money off them as I can."

"It's been fun, but this place is a no joy." I mean it sucks; I would be a fool to come back, just because I can't keep my zipper up."

Yes I agree with you it is the first sensible thing you said, far a long time.

We went in the yard after dinner, and did our little walk about as usual, then sit down, and watch the others as they go around in little groups.

There was a group of three men sitting by themselves; every day, and one sitting by himself in the middle, with a gap between them.

And then a gap with two more on his right, the two sat on his left, was talking to each other.

But the rest sat there like birds on a wire.

When they got up for a walk, they were walking in the same formation with about the same of space between them.

What was strange, everyone move out of there path, as soon as they approach them.

It was plain to see who the leader was.

When they pass us, I look at the one in the middle, and he at me, but said nothing.

I notice 'Ron, look down on the ground every time they came close to us, or we close to them.

I notice all the inmates did the same.

Do you know who they are? "Stay away he said, they are bad news waiting to happen."

You don't want to know them, the less you know them the better off you are, and believe me the healthier you will stay.

Walking back to the cell this inmate bump into me and try to make out it was my fault. He was mad; he was ready to jump all over me, we stood there eye balling each other for a while, then he said be more careful next time, and you I said, and we kept right on eye balling each other for a while.

I don't know what I did; it seems my look was enough, he back down, after he really looks into my eyes. Sorry he said, and walks away.

That's "Okay," no problem I said, politely, and I walk off without looking back.

'Jim. Yes 'Ron.'

"Did you see the size of those arms on that bastard?" If he grabs you, he would crush the shit out of you," Man he could put out your lights in a second."

I don't think so 'Ron, he was afraid of me, he is a muscle bound puff, been lifting two much weight in the yard, he must have been in here a long time, I said.

He had nothing to do but and pump iron, because he thinks it cool.

'Jim, are you afraid of anyone?' Yes me. 'Come on.' Come on what I said, you ask me and I told you, I am afraid of me.

'Why you he said?' Because I don't know what I would do if someone back me in corner, that's why. Does that answer your question? 'No he said.'

'Ron. Why are you asking me all these, questions? "Because I saw the way you look at the Boss." Who is the Boss? "He is the guy you ask me about in the yard."

"Were you afraid of him?" No, I don't know him, so why should I be afraid of him.

He starts to say something else. "Forget I ask he said,' then he said something about the inmate with big arm." I took no notice of what he said.

'Ron, do me a favour? What he said? Talk about your favourite subject. "What's that?" You mean you don't know what that is.

Man they wear skirts.

'Oh, hell he said, she is going to call me soon, and he ran off.

I went back to the cell and start to check the result I got from my tutor.

Looking at the dates, my heart skips a beat as I say out loud, seven months and two days.

I've been here seven months and two days, I repeat, in this blasted hell hole already.

I could no longer check my work; I a sudden feeling of depression came over me.

So I lie on my back and look up at the ceiling, but this did not help.

I got up and went for a stroll to see if there is anything new or if I miss anything.

Somehow I find when I walk close to the wall and look down on the floor and wall in the corner, it takes away the feeling, of being "totally" hopeless, because I only see the floor and the wall, and it makes the place look less like a cage.

I did this most days then go for a shower, for something to do.

I always meet the same three guys with the "tattoos" every time.

Maybe they stroll around looking for something to do just like me.

Are they just walking around to ease the tension of been locked up just like me, so after a while I did not take any notice of them.

As soon as I walk into the cell 'Ron was ready to tell me about his phone call.

"She is going to have me back he said, punching the air with his fist, and jump up and down."

'Ron, you can tell me when I get back I am going for a shower.

I got my towel, soap and shaving kit and hurry out before he start to tell me because I know he would be at it for a long time.

As I enter the toilet, I saw the same three inmates again, the ones with the tattoo's.

'Ron told me there names 'Lonny, 'Brian, and 'Stan.

66

"They are wired-does he said.' Ron was right they look really weird with all the "tattoos."

There was very little space on their arms where there was no tattoo's, man they look as heard as nails, I thought as I pass them.'

I look at them, with a quick glance as usual, and thought no more about them.

'As I walk into the shower room and take off clothes, suddenly I was grabbed, from behind and my arm force up my back.

Then 'Brian, hit me in the gut several times and also in my face, splitting my lip.

There was nothing I could do; I was caught completely off guard with my clothes off.

When I woke up I was in hospital.

I could see just an out line of a person sitting by my bed; it was 'Lisa, she said something. But I took no notice, because I was hurting all over, my lips, felt num, and I had a horrible ringing in my ears. She presses the bell button.

The nurse came and then the doctor, 'lay still he said,' as he check my pulse.

I went back to sleep, I don't know why.

A few hours later I woke, Lisa was still there.

What I am doing here I ask? And try to move, don't move she said in a quiet voice, I'll get the doctor.' She presses the bell button. What happen I ask? My mouth hurts.

The doctor will tell you.

"My name is doctor, 'Mann, he said."

"Stays still, "don't" move about two much and he took my pulse."

Again, I ask what happen to me doc. "Are you sure you want to know?" Yes doc.

"Promise me you will stay very still if I tell you." Okay doc. I whisper.

"You have two broken ribs, broken arm, split lip, broken nose, and two black eyes," And as far as we know, you were rape several times." Tears came to my eyes.

I start to move.

The nurse hand him a needle, and he quickly stuck it in my arm.

'Lisa got up and walks away; she could not take what she was hearing.

When she came back there were still tears in her eyes and her nose was red.

She sat down, but said nothing.

Doctor how long will I be in here? "About two maybe three weeks, don't worry about that now."

"Your ribs are the worse; we had to operator to put them right."

"You broke those ribs recently haven't you?" Yes doc. I did not explain how.

'Just "don't" move around two much, and you will be alright he said." Thanks doc I said.

"See you later he said," remember stay calm."

Pulling her chair closer to my bed she yarned, I should get in bed with you she said, 'you would think I did not get any sleep last night," she gave a sly smile."

I dare you; I said and smile back.

I was trying very hard to hide the feeling that I was burning up inside, and that I was getting ready to kill some one.

"Do you want some more broken ribs she said?" No thanks; 'well that's what you will get, if I get in bed." Are you that good I said joking? And she starts laughing. "Jim. That would be telling."

I can't believe it; I miss my chance taking you to bed just because I have a couple of broken ribs I said.

Want to hear something funny I said? 'What she said?' You are the best lawyer I ever had.

But I will be honest; I hope you are the last.

But thank you for been here, at least if I die someone will turn up to see them plant me.

'Jim, I know you don't want to talk about it; "can you remember the faces of the people who attack you?" Yes I can.

Well when you feel better, there will be someone from the prison and the police coming to ask you some questions; "don't" be afraid to tell them everything "Okay."

I did not answer; instead I close my eyes and grind my teeth.

"Are you alright she ask?" Yea I am fine. "Want the doctor?" No I am fine.

You are loosing a lot of time from work aren't you, I said changing the subject.

"Not really I book a few days off."

What a way to spend your holidays visiting a jail bird.

"Stop it you are not a jail bird," don't ever let me hear you call yourself that again."

'Jim, it doesn't bother me so, "don't" let it worry you," I wish I could come to see you more often."

'Lisa, I am not the type of person for you to spend two much time with,' you won't be a lawyer for long if you keep coming to see me.

If the news papers get to find out you spend a lot of time with me, you will get the type of head lines you don't need.

Things, is not going to get better. "What do you mean by that she asks?" 'Lisa, my life is on a down hill run without brakes can't, you see.

"Jim, don't worry about that now," think about getting better first," and then work on how to stop the down hill run."

'Jim, think positive please rise above this place please, 'I beg you."

"Sorry I have to leave you,' I have a long drive, and some work I have to do when I get home." See you tomorrow 'Okay.'

She gave my good hand a little squeeze, and turn to go, and then stop.

"Don't" worry about the news papers I am your lawyer and I have the right to visit you, as often as I want 'Okay.'

I lay there thinking why Me.

Then I was suddenly taken over with a feeling of anger.

For the first time in my life I could kill, really kill and ask questions after.

Right then and there, I start to plan my revenge; I decide I was not going to let anyone take advantage of me ever again.

And that I would do whatever it takes to let them remember me for the rest of there lives.

I promise myself there will never be a day that they will get up and don't remember me.

Just like I will remember them for the rest of my life, I know it won't be easy to get revenge because I am in prison.

Even if it kills me or if I spend all my life in prison, I will never let them get away.

Suddenly I did not care how long I spent in prison.

I must plan every move without anyone knowing that I plan to carve them up.

As I lay in bed hurting, I want to get up, and I want to lie down,' I could not decide what was best for me. Sometime I think death would be a relief.

There is no way to "describe" how I feel. I could not sleep so I told the male nurse; and he gave me a sleeping tablet.

After a while I fall a sleep but as soon as I wake the first thing that came into my mind is revenge.

I was thinking of every possible way to get even, it was slowly driving me mad.

When I look down the passage 'Lisa was coming as soon as she saw me there was a big smile on her face.'

She greets me with a hand shake and in a soft voice asks me if I was feeling better.

"Then she looks at me very serious and asks what the problem was?" Nothing I said.

"You look worried." No I am fine. "Are you sure?" Yes. "If you have something worrying you please let me know?" No everything is fine.

She places a bag on the table; "here are some goodies for you," when you feel like eating." Thanks.

"Is there anything special you would like me to bring you?" No thanks.

"Is there anything you want to tell me she asks again?" No I am fine.

"Are you going off me then?" Not in a million years. "Good that's nice to know."

"So what is the matter?" I am fed-up been in here that's all.

I was so fill with anger, and the only thing I could think of was revenge.

I think she suspect that I am very angry, even though I try to hide it.

"Have they been to interview you yet?" What for I ask? "I told you the police would come to see you," so they can find the inmates who assault you?" No they don't care; I am guilty again, I should not have a shower by myself, I have no rights.

"She looks at me very serious; I'll chase them tomorrow.

'Lisa, can you tell me if they are fond guilty what will the courts do to them? "They will put them down for a long time."

How long is a long time? "I don't know it depends on the judge."

What six months I ask? 'Could be more, why she asks?' It's Okay I just want to know. "Don't worry about that; just get well, your appeal should come up soon."

"What do you think they will do, will they let me go?" "I don't know, but they will ask you a lot of questions and then decide."

"I'll be honest with you; you never can tell what they will do."
So the chance of getting out is almost zero.
"No it all depends on how they view your behaviour since you been inside."
"They will take other things into account also."
Other things, such as, I ask? There was a long pause.
"Let's not worry about that now; you have enough on your plate already, without worrying about what may, or may not happen."
'Lisa, if you want to get your life mess-up keeps coming to seeing me.

My life is in the cess- pit right now and its going to get worse; there is no way you can get away from the stench.

If the news papers find out you comes to see me, your face will be all over the front page, and that is not the type of publicity you want.
'Jim, I told you not to worry about me I am your lawyer,' I told you; I can come to see you as often as I want.'

"What do you mean it's going to get worse?" You said that before." It's just a figure of speech.
"Don't' you do anything stupid, Jim promise me you won't take the law into your own hands, and dish out your own punishment," Jim that would be stupid."
'Lisa, all I can promise you is from now on I'll defend myself, I'll fight to the death; I can't let people walk all over me anymore.
She went very quiet for a while.

I spoke to the doctors; they say you are doing well, and that you will be out of here very soon.
"Jim, I am sorry this is the last day I can come to see you."
"But I will ring you everyday while you are still in here."
Thank you for coming I will miss you.
'Lisa, I said and holding my breath, searching for the right words, it took me so long.
'She said 'Jim, I never know you could be shy." me shy no I am not I was just searching for the right words.
"Go on take your time, I won't interrupt you again." Are you sure? "Yes I am."

71

Well here we go close your eyes, you know the nurse you tell me to love I fond her.

Her eyes pop open, you lie you don't mean that old battle axe, "impossible."

And why not I ask? "That's not your type." How would you know my type? "You would be surprise if I tell you."

And what is your type please tell me? I was trying to get her to say me. 'I will tell you next time, I don't have time now; I got to run." I have to meet someone in about thirty minutes, and I am running late already."

Are you going to meet your boy friend? "No I don't have one." Why? "Let's say I am choosy."

When she reach the door, she wave goodbye with just her long fingers.

As she walks through the door, I found myself thinking how to even the score with, 'Brian, 'Lonny, and 'Stan.

I have to let them suffer as much as I am suffering, I whisper to my self.

They must remember me for the rest of there life, just as I will remember them, I said almost out loud.

I want them to live with the memory of what I done to them, just, as I have to live with memory of what they done to me.

Extra time in prison means nothing to them; they will do the time and forget it like it was yesterday's dinner.

I was so deep in thought, when the doctor came, I did not know until he picks up my hand to check my pulse.

'Take off your top please he said, let's check your ribs, he checks my nose.

My arm was still in plaster; 'Okay he said you'll be fine,' you can go back tomorrow.

We will take the plaster off in the morning before you leave. Thank, you doc.

When I got back to my cell, 'Ron was there he look at me, but he couldn't look me in my eyes. It was as if he was embarrassed, knowing what they did to Me.

'Are you Okay he asks?' Yea, I am fine. He did not say anything for quite while.

It was as if asking me questions was taboo, so we sat there not speaking for a long time.

Then I ask how you are. I am Okay he said.

72

Good did you miss me I ask smiling? He smiles back.

"Like a hole in the head he said." That's nice to know.

'Jim. Yes. "We know who attack you."

Don't worry about it 'Ron, let it go, the less said the better.

"Jim, everyone in here knows who done it." Ron, please let it go, it's alright.

Don't say anything, and if anyone asks you if I say anything, about who attack me tell them I said I don't know.

"Why, 'Jim?" Because I want them to feel they got away with it.

So remember if you are asked, just say I don't know who done it to me, Tell them I lost my memory.

This is important, don't say anymore. Remember I don't know who attack me.

Say I say can't remember.

'Ron, I mean it, please do as I ask.

'Why?' 'Ron, I said, I do not know who beat the crap out of me.

Can you understand that? "Okay," "okay," I heard you but I don't understand."

He sat and looks at the floor, for quite a while.

Come on let's go for a walk in the yard; as I enter the yard, all the inmates stare at me.

Some even turn to others and point saying that's him.

I calmly went about my business, taking no notice of them, I did not show any feeling; I walk about like I own the place, as if nothing happen.

After a week the staring got less and the whispering stop, it was now stale news.

When I meet Brian, and his pals, I ignore them, they were sure they got away with it, because I was scared of them, and that I was not going to do anything.

But my anger did not leave me.

Every night I came up with a different idea how to get even.

But when daylight came my plan was no good, they were all bound to fail.

But I never give up trying to find a way to get even.

There were nights, I thought I was going mad, asking myself in the dark how I can trap them.

The days turn into weeks and then two months, but they never let me forget it, everyday they look at me, as if I was a "piece" of shit.

And it was plain to see; given half the chance they would do it again.

But worse of all the people who is suppose to look after my safety, did nothing but ask a few questions.

It was as if it did not happen, ever time I pass Brian, Lonny and Stan, they would laugh saying, man you was a good screw, please can we have some more.

Every time they say this, I feel like I was back into a corner; I was trying very hard not to loose my sanity.

I held myself back from jumping on them, thinking my day will come; I will wipe the smiles off your faces.

I was holding on to the rags of life, and it got harder each day, as I try to wring out every drop of courage I could find, to survive one day to the next.

Then one day when waiting in line to get dinner, it came to me how I can get even.

And wipe that smile off the bastards face forever.

My plan was so simple, I could not fail.

So I plan every move one step at a time for a few days. Then I spent a lot time watching them especially in the dinning room.

In my cell I practice swinging to my left, and back to my right, and back to my left as fast as I could for days. I practice this over and over, with a book in my hands.

When I swing to my left I drop the book, and then swing to my right, and stab out with my right hand, and then I swing back to my left, I grab my bed and pull heard.

I need a weapon, what I can use for a weapon, over and over I ask myself what I can use, that once I am finish with it they would not know what I use.

I did not want anyone to know what I use to do the job.

That's when I decide my weapon, would a pencil, so I sharpen, the point like a wedge, and I carry two pieces with me everyday.

Going into dinner everyday I make sure 'Ron went in the line before me and that he was always at least six feet in front of me.

As I got my dinner, plus a nice bowl of hot soup, as I fill the bowl my heart skips a beat, and my hands start to shake a little.

Then I reach into my pocket took out my pencil, and hold it under the tray, in my right hand.

'Ron, walk away before me, and I gave him a good start, when I reach the table where 'Brian, Lonny and Stan sit everyday for there meal, I empty everything on the tray, including the tray with the hot soup into Lonny's face. He jumps up screaming.

Then I swing to my right as fast as I could, with my pencil, stabbing 'Brian in his eye.

He grabs his face jump up screaming my eye my bloody eye; you stab me in my fucking eye.

With blood running between his fingers, he kept spinning round and round like a headless chicken.

While he was screaming 'Lonny was jump up and down screaming, fucking hell, trying to brush off the hot soup and dinner that I spill all over him.

He was so busy trying to brush off the hot food, and at the same time trying very hard to rip his shirt off, he took no notice of me, or what I did to 'Brian.

So I grab him by his testacies and pull him from between the table into the passage.

Slipping on the soup when I got him out into the passage, he fell on the floor, with me still holding his testacies; I was holding them so tight he starts to vomit.

As I plunge the pencil several times into each of his testacies and blood start to pour through the trousers cloth as I let it go.

In the meantime 'Brian starts to move up the passage between the rows of table's, trip over 'Lonny, and me and fall.

I move quickly over 'Lonny, and stab him in one of his eye, he was like a piece of meat on the floor, when I stab him in the eye, he did not move, so I don't think he felt it.

I quickly grab 'Brian, by his testacies, and stab him several times in them, while he was trying to get up.

When I grab his testacies I pull down hard on them and stab him several times then let go.

He roll-over and went to sleep like a baby.

Making sure he could never use them again, I got up and shout as loud as I could, now let me see you use those again you son of a bitches.

75

You bastards now I know you will remember your last screw, as long as you live.

I was covered in blood, and 'Stan was standing there looking dazed, with his mouth wide open, he could not believe what he was seeing, so I went after him very quick.

Suddenly he snaps back to life, when he realizes I was coming for him.

He jump unto the table and ran, along the table stepping, into the other inmate's food all along the table, and fell just before he reaches the end of the tables.

I try my best to get him, but I could not get through the other inmates who were all standing up to see what was happing.

Everything went smooth, just as I planned it, I did not get all three of them, but I was very please, I was so happy tears fill my eyes, It was like a dream come through.

I look at them on the floor; as I pass them, just laying there with blood everywhere.

I leave them just like they left me in the toilet on the floor. Some inmates were standing on the tables, and in the passage; the guards were running from everywhere.

Trying to get through the inmates, to see what it was all about, and to stop it.

It was over so fast there was nothing to stop, but there was a lot to clean up.

When the inmates saw me coming towards them covered in blood they step aside and let me walk out the door.

'Brian, and 'Lonny, were still on the floor out cold when a guard got to them, and shout someone call the doctor, call the fucking doctors and the ambulance now.

Call the ambulance now, and then another guard shout again, even louder.

I walk out slowly between the inmates and out the door, I went for a shower.

I was trembling so much I could hardly stand up; I found myself thinking now I done something, let them do their worst.

When I finish showing I went back to my cell and lay down, a few minutes later two screws came for me, truncheons in hand. 'Pick up your stuff now.' I pick up all my books, and follow them. They took me to another cell, and lock me in.

Just before they walk away one screw said you got even, you did, didn't you? Man you got even in a big way, you are lucky; you did not kill the son of bitches.'

"You are a dangerous son of a bitch; you are bloody crazy do you know that?" Man you are a crazy son of a bitch.

"How do you expect to get away with it?" I did not answer.

"I did not say this, the screw said; they deserve what you done to them." We heard what they did to you," it was disgusting, but you have a huge problem now."

What problem I ask? "The governor won't think it's funny; he will be jumping on you so hard you will wish you were dead."

You know what screw, you go and tell the governor tell him I don't care, go and tell him now, that I said I don't care.

How about some food I ask? I did not have anything to eat.

"How can you eat after what you just did?" Let me worry about that.

"I'll try to get you something." Thank you.

They turn to go and stop. 'You don't look worried?' Why the hell should I? They did not worry about me, so why the hell should I worry about them.

'What else can the law or anyone do to me that those assholes haven't done already?' I hope the sons of bitches, don't die; if they do that would spoil it.

'Why?' It would be two easy for them; I want them to live, so they will have something to remember for the rest of their lives.

Instead of just gloating over what they done to me, from now on every time the son of a bitches look into a mirror with one eye, they will remember me until the day they die.

Just, like I remember them.

'Ha, well one screw said as long as you are ready to face the music, I suppose it's alright.

It was very late when they bought me something to eat, but I ate it.

Is there any news I ask? 'No but they say you done a good job on both of them.'

What was left of there balls the doctors remove them, and the both of them have one eye now.

'They will need a black patch over it, or a glass eye.

Everyday when I was not studying I slept, I made up for the sleep I lost thinking how to get even, I was so relax, and please with what I done, I slept like a baby every night.

I was still half a sleep, when the cell door opens, get up this voice said and put your hands on your head, turn your back a guard said.

I did, but ask what for; "you're going to see the governor."

On the way to see the governor, all the inmates shout you done well nut cracker.

Everyone was calling me nut the cracker; to the inmates I was famous,

I saw 'Jerry, as he shout 'Jim, it's me, I nod, see you later he shouts, as if we were long lost friends.

The guards and I walked into the governor office. "So you are the famous nut cracker he said, looking up from the papers he was reading about me, and what makes you think you can get away with taking the law into your own hands, and dishing out your own punishment, in my prison. I just look at him.

He turns another leaf, 'that's five nuts you crack, he mumbled who the hell do you think you are? I could see a slight smile on his face when he said it, as he turn his head away very quick; to stop me seeing that he wanted to laugh.

I could see he was holding back from laughing out loud, as his shoulders start to shake, and his head went backward.

Then he turns and faces me looking very serious, "maybe they deserve what you did, but this time you fuck up," you really fuck up haven't you?" You well and truly fuck up."

Sir I said with no disrespect your language is as bad as mine.

He glares at me, "you think this is funny do you?" Yes sir I don't care what you are anyone do to me.

"Because they won't think it's funny anymore."

Sir they are lucky my other choice was to kill them.

"You put this establishment in all the news papers," on Tele, and the radio, everybody is talking about it.

The news papers are lining up out side to get a photo of you.

"Have you got any idea what you done?" Yes sir it's no worse than they done to me.

Sir the whole world will know they can't fuck me and get away with it.

One thing for sure they won't want to screw anymore, will they sir? He did not answer.

78

But from the expression on his face I could see he wanted to say something, but he couldn't say it.

As he slowly turns each sheet of paper in the folder, he was reading about me,' he comments, you are a hard case aren't you?" No sir, I won't let people take advantage of me, no matter what the consequence; I will face that when I come to it.

"Don't you think we know who took advantage of you?" "We have DNA samples, and other evidence, we plan to deal with it after we get all the fax?' Sir dealing with it the laws way, do you know what the law will do to them?" They will give them another six months, and tell them not to do it again; do you think that's fair?" I have to live with what they done to me the rest of my life.

There will never be a day that they won't remember what I done to them, I got my revenge. So as far as I am concern, the punishment fits the crime.

They will remember me first thing in the morning and the last thing at night.

He said nothing.

Sir I can live with what I done, because I know every time they look into a mirror, they will see a black patch, where they had an eye, and when they take out there pricks, it will be a dead prick.

The only thing they can use their prick for is to have piss, I know they will remember me for the rest of there lives, because they have two vital organs missing.

I wish I could have done more, but just known their sex life is gone for ever is good enough for me.

Sir the only thing they have left now is memory, and I am at the top of the list that's for sure, it makes me feels good, I feel so good I don't care what the court does to me.

I am happy to do six months more, this time it is for something I did.

"Don't tell me you are still claiming you did not break into that shop."

Warden that is still my story, and I know one day the truth will come out, my only hope is, I don't have to spend six years in here, before they catch the bastard who done it.

He opens a large, envelop and pull out a folder with my photos, his face cringe.

79

He closes his eyes, and closes the folder, and then he took a deep breath, looks at me but said nothing. After a while he opens the folder it again.

"Take him back, he can go back to his cell don't lock him up, I don't think he is going anywhere." Yes sir he said.

'And take the cuffs off now.' Thank you sir I said.

"As I turn to go, he said wait it a minute, keep out of trouble, you done enough."

I did not answer. As I start to move again, "did you hear me?" Yes sir. Good because if I hear you sneeze, and someone complains, you will wish you were never born."

Who the hell does he think he is I say out loud, as the screw lead me from his office? "You better do as he says; he can make life real bad for you."

It's all right for him; nobody is taking advantage of him.

He is not lock-up for something he did not do. So you hear me, I promise if anyone even looks at me two long, I will be going after them so fast, if the warden is in the way I will roll right over him.

"You think you are a hard case "don't" you?" Well the warden knows how to deal with hard cases."

I don't know what your name is? "It's 'Jack." 'Okay' Jack, if you were me, and some funny people, decide to take advantage of you, what you would do? 'I would report it."

Jack it's too late to report anything. "Why he ask?" They 'don't' tell you they are going to do it; they just do it and leave you wishing you were died.

And then they laugh at you and the warden after they done it.

They don't care a shit what the warden thinks, or what he will do them, because six more months in here means nothing to them.

I have only been in here a few months now, and I see things, you won't believe me if I tell you, there are people in here who is afraid to look at some people, because they are afraid of what they will do to them.

"Don't" you think we know this?" So why don't you do something about it. 'Because this person is not breaking the law, they only break the law when they do something."

This is not going to happen to me, I will never walk away, or look down. If no one troubles me I will be a model prisoner, you wont know I am here I promise you.

When, I return to my cell 'Ron was there. "Hi nut cracker he said smiling, nice to see you are alive," I thought the warden would have you strong up by now.

I look at him very serious, where the hell did you get that from? "Get what?" Calling me nut, cracker.

"Don't blame me 'Jim, "that's" the name the news papers is calling you, also every one in here," so you better get use to it." There is not, one inmate who will trouble you now; they don't care a shit for those two bastards anyway," and I feel the same. "Jim, no one is going to loose any sleep for them, so there is no need to worry."

That evening when I went for dinner all the inmates stare at me, they look at me different, from when I came out of the hospital.

They whisper to each other, but as soon as I get close to them they stop.

'Ron and I sit at the same table we always use, 'Jerry came and asks if he could sit with us, I said if 'Ron doesn't mind. "Okay" he said.'

Right away Jerry starts to talk, and we could not get a word in edge ways.

After a while I said 'Jerry, give your tongue a rest will you.

'Sorry 'Jim, you know me I don't know when to shut up."

Well do, it now will you. "Do what?" Shut up. "Okay 'Jim.'

I look up and I saw 'Stan, getting ready to sit in his usual seat, I got up, and he saw me.

So he put the tray down with his food and walks out.

'Ron, looks at me what's up?" Nothing I said.

Some of the other inmates saw what he did but said nothing.

Instead they look at me, knowing I was going after 'Stan, they all kept quiet and pretend they did not see.

As we walk out the dining hall, 'Stan, was standing behind a column waiting to go back to eat.

'Stan, did the same thing everyday, he would wait behind the column until I eat, and walk out.

Someday he barely made it; I start to wonder if I would ever catch up with him, so once again I start to make plans how to trap him.

We went into the exercise yard as usual and walk around for a while, as I sat down in my usual spot; two inmates came over to us.

One look at 'Ron, and 'Jerry, beat it he said.

'Ron did not move fast enough, did you hear I said beat it now.

81

I stood up, who the hell do you think you are? They move closer to me, looking very menacing.

I though here we go again, some more asshole looking for trouble, 'then a voice behind them said no," and they move a side and he step forward.

I recognize him but I did not know his name, because 'Ron said the less you know them the better off you will be.

Who are you I ask? It doesn't matter he said. Well I don't speak to people who don't matter. He looks "annoyed" but brushes it off.

"All you need to know is I am on your side," Why? What is in it for you? Or what do you want? 'I want nothing from you."

Well that nice to know, because I have nothing.

'You done a good job on 'Stan's, friends, I admire a man who knows what he wants,' and do what he wants to, and do it good." But your job is not finish; you still have to do the last asshole to finish the job, and I think you need to get even with Stan; I can set him up for you."

Again I ask what is in it for you, and why would you want to help me? 'No wonder they call you the nut cracker, you are a hard one to get to."

"I said I want to help, that's all, and I said I want nothing for my services." You see those five guys?" Yes I see them why? "If I nod, or say yea, or snap my fingers they will roll over you like a steam roller," they "don't" have to kill you, to prove my point; I can make you spend a long time in hospital, and every inmate will see them roll over you and they will not say a word to anyone.

They will let you live because all they will to do is break your back and mess up your spine.

'Oh, hell that could be bad, for my health I said smiling, why would you want to do that, you don't know me, and I haven't done anything to you? He looks at me; 'I "don't" need to know people.

So tell me what have I done to you I repeat? 'Nothing he said.

"But if you refuse my help and it gets around it would not look good for me would it."

Why? I don't need to explain that he said.

Sorry I need you to explain to me why.

'Because I don't want to get myself mix up with something I don't know about, that I may regret later.

"Don't worry about it he said, there will be no strings attached," I just want to help you get even with 'Stan."

I hate those types of people, if they want to do things like that they should find one of there own kind."

"They make me sick.' He deserves the same faith as the others," and you deserve your revenge."

"Okay" set it up; I'll be there, as long as you don't want anything type of payment in return. "I'll ask nothing of you, I promise." Remember I said I have nothing; this seems to annoy him when I repeat it, but again he said I want nothing.

"I see it like this, you can do the same to him as you done to 'Brian, and 'Lonny, or get him I to spill the beans."

What do you mean spill the beans? "Squeeze him very hard and he will tell you everything he knows, that's what I mean."

"So when you go to back to court you will have a few chips to play with," because the judge will want to know why you castrate those two bastard." You cannot use revenge as an excuse, if you say you did it because they hurt you the judge will slap you with another year.

"You know what I mean; it's up to you what you do to him, I am not going to tell you how to deal with it," but use your head, don't just dive in and carve him up, make it work for you; get as much information out of him as you can," get him to tell you everything he knows about the others."

"That is the best way to do things, let it work for you."

"He is the only one that will tell the truth now, because he has a lot to loose, and he is shit scared of you; so he will grab any offer that you give him that shows him a way to save his nuts." Thank you I said.

"Before you go, what ever you do, I "don't" know anything about you and 'Stan, because if he dies it's your neck remember that, last but not least, don't chase him any more, let him feel safe; let him feel like he got away with it."

"If you keep chasing him he will be hard to trap, because he will be looking over his shoulders all the time to see if you are around." "Okay" I said.

He got up and his bodyguards move to his side without him saying anything.

He starts to move off and stop. 'Oh, those two fools you are with all the time say nothing to them," especially the one who can't stop talking? He is just like a dam parrot, he has no brains, but he can talk." The one you share your cell with, is just as bad."

"So if they or anyone else, including the screws ask what we were talking," just say I want to know who you are, that will stop them asking more questions."

"And don't ever tell them anything you and me disgust."

"To be safe never talk about what you are going to do."

"Don't even talk in your sleep."

Sure enough 'Ron, asks me what the Boss want? 'Ron he wants to know, who I was, and where I am from, and warn me about getting two big on his patch. "Honest"? No I am only joking.

"Jim, the Boss looks at you like just another flea on a dog in here."

"As far as he is concern you're just make up the numbers, simple put you are just a flea in here."

Thank you 'Ron, you make feel very important, you make me feel so important, I feel like going out and get drunk and bite a dog. "I think I will come with you, but I won't bite the dog."

"How are you going to do it?" Do what?

"Bite the dog?" 'Ron, first I will walk out the front gates.

"When are you going?" How, about right now? "That sounds good to me he said, and we start laughing." What I said was stupid, but at least that stop him asking questions, I was never one for answering a lot of questions.

I stop chasing 'Stan.

I did not stop suddenly; instead someday I sneak a look at him.

Then I treat him just like he was any other inmate.

This went on for two months.

I could see he was no longer watching my every move anymore; and he was sure I gave up chasing him.

Half the time he did not even look at me when we pass shoulder to shoulder.

I totally ignore him; I ignore him that much he starts to eat his meals like nothing ever happen.

But every now and them, I would catch him looking at me, because he was not quite sure he got away with it.

"Jim, are you going to crack Stan's nuts?" Why? "Well I have this strange feeling you are."

'Ron, the less you know the safer you will be, but I'll tell you the truth, I "don't" know yet, I can't make up my mind.

I would like to get him to talk, tell me everything he knows, to save his nuts.

'That's a good idea." So keep your mouth shut. "But still crack his nuts he deserve it."

'Ron, if you don't shut up I'll crack your nuts.

"No thank you, I sooner shut up."

I decide to spend all day reading my books, when a guard came to me. "You are wanted up front." 'Lisa was waiting for me.

She looks at me very serious. Then after a while she asks why? "Jim, why did you do it?" 'Lisa, I said those people abuse me, there is no way I could let them get away with it, if I did, I could not live with myself.

Not only that I have to live in here for the next five years and three months.

If I let them off, every inmate in here would think I am easy meat, and they would all walk over me, they would think lets have a quickie; he is easy he won't do anything.

At least I give them something to think about, before they try.

'Jim, you are right, but you should let the courts deal with it.

'Lisa, I thought of that, but every time I pass them, they laugh at me, they took the piss out of me everyday.

I couldn't take it any more; it was like they were raping me every time I see them, I had to stop them.

I just could not let the courts, give those bastard six months, to people like them doing six months inside is just like having a dinner break, they don't care; this place is home to them.

'Lisa, knowing my luck, they could get away with it, some stupid Judge who may be bent himself, looking at my case may think I deserve what they done to me.

She sat quiet, and took a long at me. 'Jim, that wouldn't happen.

'Lisa, the courts will have to do what they want to do to me, six months, or six more years, it's up to them.

So far no one believes I am "innocence" away from you, I done nothing wrong and here I am, sitting behind bars.

I don't care anymore, so let's see if they will give me six months.

If they do, it's worth it, just for the piece of mind I have now.

"I am disappointed 'Jim,' I was hoping you would rise above what's happening to you."

"But you are right to do what you did," its bit barbaric don't you think?

'Lisa, you could be right.

But the law is also barbaric locking me up, for something I did not do; just because I can't prove I was in bed.

But they believe the old man when he said he saw me.

There is another way to look at it, if they did not put me in here; if they did not cerate the little hell I am living in, I would not be in this position.

'Lisa, I am very sorry I let you down, that is all I can say.

"You did not let me down; I can understand how you feel now I that I talk to you."

"But I still say you should have let the courts deal with it."

'Lisa, most women can't fight back when they are rape, so when something like this happens to them, they must feel "terrible" when the courts let the son of bitches off with nothing but a smack on the wrist.

As far as I am concern, they should castrate all of them that's why I decide to do the smacking myself, no matter, what the courts decide to do to me.

But at the end of the day, I still have to live with what they done to me, for the rest of my life, so all I done is even the score.

Now every time they unzip there pants, or look into a mirror, they will remember me just like I remember them.

So instead of laughing about it, they will regret it.

'Lisa, you will not believe this, when I came back here form hospital.

Those bastards they look at me everyday and laugh, they though it was funny, I bet they don't think it's funny anymore.

I wish I could turn the clock back, for your sake, but to be honest, I would do it again, just for the piece of mind I have now. I can sleep nights now, I sleep like a baby.

I wish I could do it again, just to make sure I done a good job.

'Jim, the doctors say you done a good job."

Thank you.

My only thought now is when this nightmare going to end, that's why I must learn to live one day at a time now.

I must be very careful; I do not trust anyone in here any more.

If I live to get out, trusting the police again will be very hard. 'Jim, I don't know what this will do to your "appeal" they may decide not to give you one.

"They will say you're two "violent" to let out, they will think you should have let the law deal with them.

You mean like they deal with me, 'Lisa, I'll be "honest" with you, I "don't" expect anything from them, even before this happen.

And it's worse now; I "don't" expect anything at all, I "don't" even expect them to come and see me.

My only hope now is that the guy who broke into the shop does it again soon, and they catch him.

I think that is only chance I have to get out of here early.

Believe me; I am very glad I did not kill them, I was so mad I could have killed them, and walk away laughing.

You heard enough of my problems how are you? "I am fine."

"And you she said smiling?" Well I have seen better days.

May I ask you one question I said? "Yes what." Then she said, quickly hold on.

"You ask that question before."

Okay since you like that question so much can I repeat it? "You may," but I still "don't" have an answer for you."

Jokingly I said what question we are talking about. "Bed she said and smile."

Ha well I said, this is turning out to be one of my better days.

Why she asks?' Well for starters you did not say no, "that's" why.

Does that mean you are thinking about it I ask? "Can we change the subject please?" Why I ask? Have you got something against talking about bed? She, pause and look at her watch, "doesn't" time fly when you are having fun."

Are you going to give me an answer? "No you are good at working things out," so work it out for yourself."

'Lisa, you know I am going to loose a lot of sleep thinking a bout it. "Well a least I know what you will be thinking about when I am not with you."

Is that bad I ask? 'No, but remember you are in a cage."

Thank you for reminding me.

"I" better leave now before I say something I don't want to say."

'Lisa, do you know you always run away? "Yes I know that's what keeps me safe."

Safe from what I ask? "Bye Jim I'll come back to see you soon." When? "I don't know."

"Since you enjoy my company so much I'll try and make it as soon as possible." "Remember I am a working girl; I can't just drop everything and come to see you."

Well at least I have something to look forward to.

"She reaches the door and return to the table."

Back so soon? "Yea 'Jim, you and I have to have a serious talk, I have to get you out of here," and the only way it is going to happen is through an appeal," so please "don't" do anymore damage to your case, or anyone else, will you."

"If anyone is stupid enough to attract you, please walk away," please will you? 'Lisa, please do not worry about me, they all know me and what I am capable of, so they will either kill me or stay away. "Jim, that's not funny." Sorry.

You want to know something, this is very funny, when I walk in the passages now, or they pass me anywhere, everyone move out of my way.

They keep as far as possible away from me, It makes me feel like I have a very deadly disease, or I smell.

I don't mind what the hell they do, as long as they keep away.

"Okay" remembers what I say, keep out of trouble."

"Bye for now, see soon."

'Lisa, I said. She stops, and looks at me.

"What is it this time?" I still love you I whisper, so be good.

She smile came back to the table.

And whisper you can't love your lawyer I told you that is stupid."

When I return to my cell, and I start to read my book, a guard told me to go and pick up my parcel, your lawyer leave it he said.

It had a lot of new books, and the result of the work I sent, the month before.

I made a lot mistake, so the tutors ask me to do them again.

I start to check all the wrong ones, when 'Ron came in and sits down; "are you having a nice day or a bad day?" Not bad why

"What did the Boss want?" 'Boss, who is the 'Boss, I ask? Pretending I did not know.

You know," Jim, you know who I am talking about," his cronies told me to leave."

"What, he did not tell you his name?" No. "Did you ask him?" No.
"I am not "surprise" he never tells anyone his real name."
"So what did he want?" He wants to know, if I am "Okay," and said I have a lot of guts, doing what I did, he thought I done an excellent job.
'Ron, I told you before what the 'Boss, want.
"No you only said he wanted to know where you came from." Lying to him was easy.

"Watch him 'Jim." "I would not trust him if I were you, if the stories I hear about him is true," he could have you killed in here, or out side and get away with it," he is bad news."
"The people around him would do it, and walk away; they will leave you like a piece of shit on the ground."
"Don't trust him 'Jim.' Watch your back when you are with him," and don't promise him anything, nor let him do anything for you, he is the type if he does you a favour he wants one back."
"I'll say it again he is bad news."
'Ron, I can't afford any more trouble, I don't want to die in here or out there, but I will use the devil to get me out of here, if that is the only way.
"That means, he has asked you to do something for him?" No he "hasn't" asked me to do anything yet."
'Jim, he will ask you, and when he does, he will wrap you up so tight you can't say no to him."
'Jim, he thinks no one have the right to say no to him, so don't let him get his claws into you."
"I should not be telling you this; I am putting myself in danger if anyone hears me,' so whatever you do "don't" repeat what I tell you."
"There is about three more people missing right now, and no one knows where they are." "Everyone suspects the Boss has something to do with it, but they can't prove it."
"These three people went missing shortly after they arrested him; he was in here at the time so they can't pin it on him."

So why is he in here? "Well the story goes he was shopped by one of his own family member," for beating a guy senseless."
"The guy is a live but he is a cabbage," they say he would be better off dead, because he can't even fart for himself, much less wiping his ass, his hands is shaking so much he find its hard to control them."

"Since then I heard of two of the same family suffer the same faith out side," but they can't pin it on him, because he is in here."

"The family swore he has something to do with it, but they can't prove it either."

They say the person he uses to do the job comes from abroad some-where, but this cannot be proven either."

"So Jim be careful don't trust that son of a bitch."

He must be one cleaver son of a bitch, I remark.

Where is he from? "Jim I don't know," and I don't and I don't want to know."

"What difference does it make 'Jim?" All I know he is a big time crook, he is into everything."

"Now that I tell you, I am going back to being stupid."

"I hear nothing, I see nothing, and speak nothing."

Thanks 'Ron, I will remember to watch my back. "Hell Jim you need to watch more than your back with this guy, you need to stay away from him, while you are in one "piece."

'That's' when I start to look at 'Ron, from a different angle; he must have heard things when he was conning women, so I did not doubt what he was saying..

He did not ask about 'Lisa, I was glad, because I did not feel like explaining what she said to me.

The 'Boss, I said out loud, that's who he is," he really looks like the 'Boss.

Looking at him he did not look like an inmate," he's well groomed, even his prison clothes looks tailor made.

His hair neatly cut, his finger nails very clean and well manicure,' I thought he was a 'power puff," at first.

He is that well groomed, when you speak to him he makes you feel inferior.

Most of the time he spoke very quiet, but his voice "dominates" every word he says, they seem to hang in the midair letting you know he is in charge.

Everyone who comes in contact with him, even the screws treat him with respect, because he does nothing, for anyone to see.

To be honest the 'Boss, does not look that scary to me, but his cronies do.

They stand out in the yard, like giant concrete pillows; just looking at them was enough to tell you keep away as far as possible.

"Ron, I said after a while, the 'Boss, is just like one of those little boys at school, in the play ground, hiding behind the big boys.

The big boys are also afraid of him, because they don't know if he will ask any of the other big boys to do a job on them.

"Jim, does that mean you are not afraid of him?" 'Ron, I don't know, so lets not talk about it.

"Well 'Jim, take a tip from me; start learning how to be afraid,' because that's the only way you will survive."

"You won't know who he will use to do a job on you; 'he is so devious he could get your mother to do you in."

Even, though 'Ron warned me about him I was not scared of him, or his cronies.

I figure if I mind my own business, and let him know where I stand from day one, I will be safe.

Who am I to complain, he is going to help me get even with 'Stan, and he said without any strings attach.

Suddenly 'Lisa's, last words came back to me,' 'Jim, keep out of trouble.

'Ha, well I'll cross that bridge when I get to it,' and start reading my books again.

'Ron, start to tell me that 'Dee, want him back," he was so excited he was like a kid with a new toy, so I stop reading and listen to him for a while.

Life became a routine after that, and it went on like that everyday for a long time.

To be honest I start to get bored.

Then one day in the exercise yard one of the 'Bosses, cronies grab my arm as I walk pass him.

"Come now he said, let's go, the boss wants you."

Hold it; I said no body grabs me, or gives orders," he lets go, the 'Boss, want you now.

"Okay" I said, but don't ever grab me again, I "don't" like people who man handles me.

Where is he? "Follow me; he was sat a few feet from the rest of his cronies, in his usual spot.

I walk towards him and two of his cronies met me halfway, turn out your pockets out, so I did, and put them back in, then he bacons me to sit

"It's on he said." It's on for tomorrow." What's on? "Stan, he said, don't you remember?" No I did not remember it's been so long I thought you forgot.

He was speaking so quiet; I could just about hear what he was saying." "There is something I think you should know," they are not the only ones involve."
What do you mean? "That's all I can say for now."

"So my advice is, "don't" carve him up straight away," let him sing first, let him spill the beans; let him say what he's got to say, it will help you if what I hear is true.
"That's" all I can tell you."
"If you decide to crack his nuts, wipe off the blade and drop it when you finish using it."
"Remember this it is important you wipe off your finger prints good before you drop it."
I can keep it and dispose of it. No I have someone who will do it for you.
Wipe off the knife if you don't the screws will trace it back to you, so wipe it good, and drop it.
'This way the screws will know you done it, but they can't prove it, because you don't have a weapon on you and there is none in the yard."
'The screws may think somebody is trying to copy you, and that will take some of the pressure off you.
"We will set him up for tomorrow, be in the yard at 2:00 pm. don't be late, and don't be early."

"We will have everything ready for you to crack two more nuts." "Don't forget his eye."
"But remember this; I don't know anything about it."
Why are you doing this? He looks at me; he did not answer my question.
"Have fun, even the score with the son of a bitch, he said."

"Boss, I am telling you this again, if your plans are to use me to do something for you later I will not do it.
"Why do you think I want something from you?" Let's put it this way,

most people want to use other people, and I am not the type to be used.

So I am telling you in advance, if you ask later you won't be disappointed, when I say no. "Jim, everyone can be used." 'Boss, you are wrong. There are some people who you can't use, and is best left alone.

"Okay" 'Jim, I will remember what you say."

Good because I would hate for us to come head to head.

"Let's not worry about that now, he said."

"Oh," one last thing when you finish the job, vanish as quick as you can out of the yard without running, don't draw attention to yourself, and clean you're self up as quick as possible, because they will be "coming" for you first.

That night I lay awake thinking, what can 'Stan, tell me that will help me? Also the quickest way I can get in and do my job, and walk out of the yard.

One thing for sure I'll not let him walk away, if what he tells me is not going to help me.

After a while, I fall a sleep and I sleep like a baby.

At one minute to two I slowly enter the yard, in the far corner I could see a small group of inmates standing close together.

I walk over, as I got up to them they let me in, and an inmate push a small blade into my hand without saying anything, I walk between them and they close the opening so no one could see me.

Then a few more move and again I walk in, again they close behind me.

'Stan was standing with his back to the wall, very calm until he saw me.

He fell to his knees.

'God no please no, please God, he said again and again.' 'Stan, it's your turn, take it like a man I said.

'He starts to shake; he was like a leaf in the wind.' 'God no please 'Jim,' don't please,' I am very sorry for what I did. 'Stan, its two late to be sorry, you should have thought of that before you screw me.

"Jim, I have something to tell you, please, don't cut my nuts please, not my nuts or eyes please."

Two inmates grab him, I'll tell you what I know 'Jim, please don't castrate me.

Please nut cracker, please "don't."

When he saw the knife tears start running down his cheeks, as he pleads,' 'Jim, there is a lot I can tell you," please hear what I have to say please."

I was all most feeling sorry for him, but I was still angry, I don't think I will ever forget what they done to me.

I found since I done the other two, most of the angry feeling was gone from me.

But I could not let him get away with what he did,' he did not feel sorry for me that day, so why should I feel sorry for him now.

If I let him go, it will get around that I gone soft.

Let's hear what you have to say, be quick about it, and it better be good.

He start to sing like a bird, one of the 'Boss, cronies wrote it all down; they gave it to him to sign and pass it around for others to sign.

You better tell it to the warden now; I'll come with you.

Don't say anything about what happen here, when we see the warden.

You say one word about what happen here and I promise next time I will take your nuts, and both eyes. Do you hear me? "Yes nut cracker." Tell the warden you want to tell the true story, because you're sorry for what you did to me.

If you mention one word of what happen out here, I promise I will do my job.

Do you hear me? "Nothing happen here."

"Okay" 'Jim, I'll tell him the full story."

'Nut cracker; I promise I won't say anything about today ever."

The 'Boss, came between his men and the others.

"You will do as he asks wont you?" Yes 'Boss.

"Make sure you here me good, if you "don't" there is not a prison you will be safe in, 'remember this." 'Yes 'Boss. I promise.' 'Okay', go with him now.

Get up now lets go.

I wipe the knife and drop it.

At the gate I ask a guard if we could see the warden.

He looks at us very long then he took us to a room.

"What is it all about he asks?" 'Stan, look at me go on tell him.

He told him, it's about the day 'Jim, got rape and beaten up.

"Wait here he said."

He went to the door, and calls two more guards, cuff them he said,' I will see if the warden will see you."

"Come he will see you now."

As we walk into his office, 'Stan did not hesitate, he told the full story, including what he did, nothing could stop him singing.

When he finishes the secretary who was writing it all down gave him it to sign.

The warden looks at 'Stan, with disgust, told the guards take this piece of shit out of my sight, lock him up," I will deal with him later."

Looking at me, he said 'I'll take it from here."

May I have a copy for my lawyer sir I ask? "Yes I will send her a copy, and ask her to come and see you ASAP."

Take the cuffs off him, he said to the other guard.

I stood there waiting to see if he was going to say anything.

"You can go he said."

"I start to move, hold on, what did you do to get him to get him to talk?" I did nothing sir.

"I don't think so; he is not the type to sing like that,' he is scared."

Look at him sir; there is not a mark on him.

"That is no proof; you must have done something to scare him." Sir I did nothing.

"Go now get out of my site before I change my mind."

Thank you sir I said, and walk out, as quickly as I could.

I went back to my cell, as I enter the cell; 'Ron, wanted to know what it was all about. 'Ron, I can't tell you anything yet, I am sorry, you will find out as soon as I know, I promise.

"What did the Boss want this time?" he didn't want anything. "It's not like him to call you for nothing."

'Ron, stay stupid please. He gave me a long look.

But he did not ask any more questions, after my remarks.

He got the message; he knew I was not going to say anything.

I start to read and do some work, suddenly my hands start to shake, knowing I came that close to carving 'Stan, up.

When this voice said hi 'Jim, hi 'Ron, 'Jerry, was standing in the door way.

Come in 'Jerry, what have you been tell the inmates about me? "Jim, I haven't said anything about you." Come on, I want the truth.

Suddenly Ron stood up; 'Jim please let me get out of here first."

'Jerry, you know what I'll do if you lie to me.

He pauses, then in a scared voice he said, 'Jim, and "hesitate."

'Jerry, I want you to sit down and tell me what you told them.

95

"I told them about what I head in the police station, that's all."

Come on what else? "I told them about detective 'Gurney;' that's all 'Jim." I told them how he beat you up," and what you did to him, before you went into hospital."

Did you add to it? 'No 'Jim I swear I didn't.' Jim don't you want anyone to know?" No I don't.' "I am sorry 'Jim, I didn't know."

"Okay", forget it, but don't say anymore, if anyone asks from now on.

Don't say anything at all. "Yes 'Jim, I mean it I'll say nothing 'Jim, I promise."

Just then two of the 'Boss, cronies turn up in the door way again."

"They look at 'Ron and 'Jerry, get lost." Ron turn stare at me before he got up and leave the cell, they walk out as if they did not have any right to be in there.

"The 'Boss, want to see you now one said."

Tell him no.

They stood there blank; as if they did not hear me.

No one ever say no to the 'Boss, before.

When I did not move he asks are you stupid?" Okay I'll tell him myself, if you are afraid to.

We walk to where he was sitting by himself in the yard as usual, but not far away was his other cronies; as usual they sat away from him so they could not hear what was said.

When we were close to him the two cronies who came to fetch me stop.

"Come he said sit here." Man I said you sure have some funny people working for you; hell they don't have any manners, they think everyone should jump as soon as you say come. 'He smile, they are only doing there job," most people I know, I have to scare them before they will do anything."

"That is why I like you, you are a known quantity," you're not afraid are you?" 'Boss, I don't mean to offend you but hear me good please. Please do not like me two much will you. "Why?" Well just between you and me, I do not bend very easy.

"What do you mean?" 'Boss, let's say you say jump, and I don't jump,' I know if I don't jump,'...' my life will be very short, being around you, but worse of all; I know others could get hurt, including you.

To tell you the truth, I do not like to see blood and I would hate to see my own again.

Let's put it like this 'Boss, I don't care anymore, and when a man doesn't care, there is not a lot anyone can do, to him.

So the only thing anyone can do to stop me is snuff me out,' and I am sure you do not want to do that.

'Jim, I "don't" think I want to do that not yet," if I reach that stage you will be the first to know."

Well I hope for both of us we never reach that stage 'Boss.

We both pause for a long time and look into space.

Then I said, 'Boss, do you know you are very funny, man you are very funny."

"Jim, I am glad you think so."

"Jim, you know that's what I like about you; I was just like you when I was your age." Okay Boss what do you want me for what is so urgent? "I just want to know how you got on that's all; did 'Stan, sing like a bird? Yes he did.

'Boss he is a good singer.

I plan to come to see you as soon as I knew more.

"What is the warden is going to do about it?"

The warden said he will take it from here, that's all he said, but for some reason I don't trust him. 'Jim, he can't walk away from this, he would loose everything if he doesn't do his job." Jim he would loose everything, if he "doesn't" take it higher; no he's got to take it all the way no matter who gets hurt.

'Did 'Stan, tell him about detective 'Gurney, and how much he is involve?' Yes, how did you know? "Let's say I know and leave it at that."

"I am glad for you; can I help you with anything else?" Yes get me out of here now.

He starts to laugh out loud.

"Now you are funny, very funny he said."

Then he asks me, what I done to get in here.

'Boss, you mean you are helping to get 'Stan and you don't know what I did.

"I herd what you done, but I like to hear it from the horse's mouth."

Are you sure you want to know? "Yea I want to know." Well I did nothing.

"Don't make me laugh he said."

Go on laugh; laugh as loud as you want. "You really mean it don't you?" Yes of course I mean it.

"Come back tomorrow and tell me all about it."

"Oh, "I am sorry please come back tomorrow he said."

He was still laughing, when I got up to walk away.

Okay what time? "Anytime you like, just tell my boys." Okay I'll do that.

It was not until I walk away that I thought how abrupt the meeting ended, and what was the reason why he suddenly, wanted me to go without saying so.

'Ha, well I whisper to myself he is strange, he is a real strange mother fucker I whisper to myself.

When I look back I could see two screws walking towards him.

I pause for a while and ponder how he knew they were coming to see him.

On my way back to the cell, an inmate stops me.

"Are you the nut cracker he asks?" Who wants to know? "My name Simon I came in this morning."

I am 'Jim." Do you want me to crack your nuts I said joking? "Heaven forbid no."

Who told you about me? "Saw your face in the news papers and on the TV."

They were on about you so much, I thought you must be nine feet tall, and weight 400lbs.

So you just came in? "Yes." How long will you be staying in this honourable establishment? I will be here for two years.

"You are the one who crack, one of 'Gurney's, nuts?" Why are you asking if you recognize me from the TV? Sorry he said.

"You would not believe 'Gurney beat the shit out me last week." So he hasn't learnt any thing from our encounter.

Man I can't believe the son of a bitch is still doing it. How bad did he beat you? "I hurt for days." Did you go into hospital? 'No.'

Well you can't prove he beat you can you? "No I don't suppose I can."

There are a lot of inmates just like you in here, why "don't" you try and find them to see; if you all can come up with something that you can use against him.

"That's a good idea I will try."

Don't tell anyone I told you to do this; I have my own problems, without asking for more.

He did not answer. Did you hear what I said? "Don't tell anyone I told you to find inmates who 'Gurney, beat. "Okay I won't."

I want you to remember that I did not tell you to seek them out, this is

98

important.

If I hear you mention my name, I promise I will crack your nuts for free.
"If I find them I'll let you know." This time I did not answer.
Instead I said good luck, and leave him.

When I got back to the cell 'Ron, and 'Jerry, was back, with their tongues hanging out wanting to know what the 'Boss, wants.
"What did the 'Boss, want this time they ask almost together."
He just wants to know how I got on with the warden, "yesterday."
"What happen yesterday, Ron asks?" 'Stan told the warden what he done to me. "Oh shit that's good Jerry said."
"Jim the 'Boss, is very dangerous that guy, watch him," don't let him get his hooks into you, I heard some strange things about him' Jerry said."
"Yea, that's what I told him yesterday."
Once again I said nothing; instead I got my books out.
Lads I am sorry, I have to get into these books, I am loosing two much time; I got a lot of work to correct, and some new ones to work out, if you don't mind.

"Why are you are you studying 'Jerry, ask again?" I thought I told you why? "No you didn't."
Well I hope someday soon I'll be leaving here, and I would like an easy job, something I don't have to work two hard at.
I bought this course before they put me in here; since I don't have to go to work.
I am trying to make the best of my time.
"Good idea I wish I could do it, 'Jerry, said leaving the cell."
Once I clear my mind of all the distraction around me, ever thing fell in place, I did all the return work, and quite a bit of the new ones.
I was surprise when 'Ron came back, and said grubs up, "aren't you going to eat today?" Yes. "Well hurry up then."

"Man those books of yours must be good, are you sure they "don't" have nude women in them?" 'Ron, we all, can't find rich women. "Yes you can." No I can't. "Yes you can."
Yes I can, I will take yours.
How is that? "No you can't." Why? "Dee is special now;" she calls me everyday."
Good for you, let's hope you are not conning her again? He took no notice of me saying he was conning her again, instead he said man I am going to stick to her like super glue.

Good I hope you mean it.

"I would like you to meet her when she comes for visits."

I don't think so.

"Why?" Hell she is coming to see you not me, it would not be fair for her to come all that way to see you, and other people turn up with you, she will want to talk to you in private, I am sure she will have a lot of questions to ask you.

I would still like you to meet her; I did not say you have to sit with us.

Okay I'll come if it's okay with her.

When is she coming? "I don't know yet, I will let you know."

The next day I went to see the 'Boss he was sitting in the same place; it was as if he never moves from that spot.

His cronies were also sitting in their usual place.

When they saw me coming they look at him, then at me, they did not say anything, or move towards me, so I went over to him, "sit here on this side he said."

I told him the full story how they put me in side.

He asks, "Do you know why they found you guilty?" No.

"The shopkeeper and his wife, that's why." They said they saw you, and from then on everyone would find you guilty, no matter who they choose for the jury."

"Even me I would find you guilty."

They did not find any finger prints; there was none of the money in my room.

They even dug up the garden and fond nothing.

There was not a single thing on me or anywhere in my room to prove I was in the shop.

So why pin the crime on to me? "Eye witnesses my dear boy," that's what they use to screw you."

"The old man and his wife really screw you," and from what you're telling me, I think that 'Gurney got them to do it," and the poor old bastards don't even realize, they done it.

"Do you want to know what made it worse for you?" He pauses; you crack 'Gurney's nut," from then on the law saw you as the villain, an evil force to lock up."

"The one thing you must not do," is crack the laws nuts," they can crack yours, but you must not crack their nut." "Hell the jury sees you as an evil asshole, someone who doesn't care a shit about the law or anyone," someone who prepare to swing a machete."

100

"Hey." They did not think for one moment you could be telling the truth," to be "honest," if I was one of the jury, I would do the same," I would not think twice, about putting your ass down."

"Is there anything I can do for you he said?" I don't think so; you still don't trust me do you?" Yes I do but I don't want to be tied to anyone. "You tied to me?" Yes.

'Boss, I do not want anything from you that will make it hard for me to say no when you ask me to do something for you, that maybe not legal.

"The expression on his face change and he looks at me very serious.

So I said very quickly, I don't mean to offend you, by saying you are into illegal things. Boss my only thought is to get to hell out of here and stay out.

"Most people don't say no to me." Boss, I know you told me once, and I can see why, but I am not like most people, I told you.

"Again he said that's why I like you."

Please don't like me two much will you I said again, this time looking him straight in the eyes.

"Okay he said if you don't want my help," so let's leave it at that, but if you change your mind let me know, I will be right here."

Thank you I said and leave, before he could say anymore.

I can't let him get his claw into me I mumble to myself I don't need any more trouble.

I don't think he is the type that will do something for nothing, either," he is a born ruler and I won't let anyone rule me.

On my way back I saw 'Ron, he was having a shouting match with two inmates.

There was a lot more shouting coming from the other inmates, 'Ron was stuck and he knew it.

Two guards were running to stop them from taking 'Ron, apart,' but I got there just before them, 'Ron, what's up I ask.

He was that afraid he could only mumble these guys are trying to rip my head off. "When the inmates saw me they say hi nut cracker, don't worry about it.

Are you sure I said? "Yea man he said;" well remember him he is my cell mate.

"See you later he said." No you don't, can you hear me? You better make sure you hear me, you don't see him later, I, mean its finish.

"Yes its finish nut cracker." Are you sure? "Yes its finish." Good.

The guards stop running because the shouting stops, they walk towards us.

"Nut cracker what's up; pardon me what was all that shouting about?" I don't know I just got here.

'Ron, do you know? "Yea I accidentally bump this guy, and he decides to rip my head off, and stuff it up my ass, even after I apologise to him."

"So nut cracker what did you do." Me I ask? I did nothing, I just show my face.

'Good he said.' Why I ask? "I can't say." Just don't get yourself into any more trouble."

Why I ask again? "Forget I said it," just keep out of trouble," that is my tip to you."

"Walk away from trouble, as far away as you can."

"Jim, why is he so nice to you?" I wish I knew. "Thanks 'Jim, for saving my bacon back there, they were about to make mince meat of me."

I herd him but took no notice, instead I was still thinking,

Why are the screws so nice? I turn to 'Ron, can you make anything sense of that I ask.

"Sense of what he asks." The screws been nice to me of all people, "nope he said screws are crazy people," they think we are mind readers," maybe they know something, and can't tell you."

When we got back to the cell I start on my books.

As I took one of the books from the box, I smell 'Lisa perfume on it.

Suddenly it felt like she was in the cell with me, I wander what you are doing I said out loud. "Who, 'Ron, ask? 'Lisa, I said. "Your lawyer he said." Yea I answered. "Why are wandering what she is doing?" About my appeal I said, the first thing that came to my mind, I did not say any more because that's not what I was thinking.

I wonder if the warden told her about 'Stan, and give her all the information.

'Ha, well it will come out in the wash, my mother use to say.

Each day seams longer will anything go right for me, I start to think that I was stuck in here forever.

Suddenly I feel like I could string myself up.

"Ron' got up are you alright?" Why I ask? 'You were making a funny sound mumbling to yourself." 'Ron, I can't take much more of this; "you will get over it, he said."

"I reach those stages myself, about three weeks after I came in here."

"It comes and goes now, but it doesn't get any easer," I am surprise it did not hit you earlier."

'I'll tell you I came very close to killing myself one night," the reason why I did not do it, is because I did not have anything to do it with."

"Thank the Lord I am over it now."

"I remember lying on the bed and shake, with sweat pouring from me," I am sure I was going mad,' believe me 'Jim, I was glad to see daylight for the first time in my life."

"I swear I would never let it happen to me again."

"I swear if I get out of here I will never come back, no matter how much money they have, I will never con another women out of a penny," but I will always beg them for a ride, because if they say yes, they can't lock me up for that, can they?" 'Jim, that night I done a lot of thinking, how can I turn things around? 'You would not believe me; somehow I just forget that night once the daylight came."

"But sometime I wonder if I was in here for life what the hell I would do."

"Jim, the only tip I can give you is do like I did."

"I think of the places I been, I think of the girls I took to bed," and the ones that got away."

"I spend a lot of time thinking, what I did wrong to let them get away."

"If you can do that, it will take your mind off your troubles for a while; mind you it will only last long enough for you to get over the worst part of the day or night."

'Ron, how long, have you got to do now? Nine more months, I assume if they gave me three years." Why assume I ask. Long story he said.

Will you be coming back for a second visit? "Man shit no, what you take me for; I am not that stupid." I am going to stick so hard to 'Dee that is my plan now."

"Hell I'll be sticking so hard, air won't get between us."

'Ron, can you remember me asking you once if you love her? You told me no, I have bad news for you; it won't work, no matter how much of a sticker you are.

How long do you think you can fool her? How long can you fool yourself into staying away from other women? I give you six months, and you will be looking for something different, to screw.

You will be looking at every piece of skirt, that past you in the street, and as soon as you do that, and she sees you that's the end of you.

She will know you are looking for a quick leg over just like before.

You, know she loves you that is why she is taking you back, so she will be watching your every move now, if she has that much money, she can get any man she wants.

The problem is she is afraid they only want her for her money just like you.

Last but not least, start choosing her money, more than her; she will know that you only want her for her money.

You are caught between the rocks and the hard place my friend so no matter how much you screw her it won't work.

He was very quiet while I was talking.

"Then he said to tell you the truth right now 'Jim, I can only see her face; there is no one else on my mind."

"I wake up in the night and she is on my mind," in the daylight she is still on my mind.

"I "don't" know if that's love, or if it is because I want her," but I can tell you this, I can't think of anything but her these days," it's like a nightmare waiting to happen." "I don't know what I would do if she found someone while I am in here."

"If you are out will you come to our wedding?" I am going to ask her to marry me." "Don't" forget I want you to meet her tomorrow," 'Jim, I have very few people who I can call a good friends so will you come to our wedding?" Yea I will, but please don't call me nut cracker," and please ask 'Dee, to call me 'Jim."

I don't know why I said yes, I "don't" really feel like been around a lot of strangers, who may ask a lot of questions?" 'Ha, well I may not get out of here in time anyway, so why worry about it.

Slowly the days turn into weeks then months.

Hell I said to 'Ron, it's over two and a half year since the son of bitches locks me up.

I was sure the asshole that broke into the shop would do it again.

"Don't worry those kind of people can't just stop; he is got to do it before long he wants to feel safe first.'

"Once he feels safe he will do it again, he knows he had a close shave the last time.

As soon as he feels safe again he will go out and try his luck. "He is not quite sure he is safe and that's why he is taking his time."

"He knows he was lucky when they pin the "robbery" on you."

"So as soon as he reaches the stage where he feels really safe, and thinks there is no one looking for him he will be at it again." Jim I believe at the moment he is not sure he got away completely, because you are in the news a lot, he thinks you may convince some one you did not break into that shop.

'Ron I hope you are right, because that's what I am hoping, and I hope he does it soon, for I can't take much more of this.

You know its bad enough if you know you done the crime; at least you know it's your fault why you are lock up, but when you know you did not do it.

That you are serving time for somebody else's crime, its hell everyday is like a life time, if I could get my hands on the son of a bitch.

"What would you do beside de nut him, and take his eyes out?" Men I don't know.

Then 'Ron, start to laugh. "I just thought of something, you could pluck his eyes out, then pull his balls off, and split the top of his prick in half, then put his balls and his eyes in his mouth," then ask him how you enjoyed that." 'Ha, very funny, I said.

What if it's a woman I ask? 'Jim, you should know better than that, a woman wouldn't break into a shop carrying a machete."

What would she carry? "I don't know."

"But if it's a woman, you could dig a very deep hole in the garden and put her in it."

What the hell for I ask again? "I don't know, I will think about it, and tell you tomorrow." Come off it tell me now.

"No I'll read you the next capture tomorrow, this is a series he said."

'Ron, do you always chat a lot of rubbish? "Rubbish yes."

"That's all I can to do in here, if I don't I will loose your marbles."

Once again the 'Boss, cronies came looking for me; and again they look at 'Ron, beat it, and as usual. 'Ron, walk away without saying anything.

Watching him go, he was just like a little puppy someone shouts at, I hope I never get like that, how horrible he must feel creeping away I thought.

But it is possible he knew something about the Boss I don't know.

So I think its best to keep quiet, I won't say anything to him about it.

I was not pleased about the way they ask me either but I went with them.

I'll tell the 'Boss, once and only once, leave me alone I've had enough.

But as I got close to him, he said I have some good news for you, before I could say anything about the way his cronies treat my cell mate.

Once he said good news everything I was thinking went out of my head. Good news? "Yes good news."

That will make a change I said smiling.

Forgetting I was angry with his cronies, I sat down very close to him, so I could hear him.

"You did not hear this from me, so do not say anything to anyone, until you hear it from your lawyers, or from the warden "Okay."

"If you say anything when you see my men next time, you'll be loosing some blood."

Thank you very much, for the bad news first.

I'll remember that when I see them coming next time to be on my guard.

"Do you still want me to tell you?" Yes. "Are you sure?" Of course I am sure.

"Okay you know the detective you de nut?" Yes 'Gurney.

What about him? "He and his partner, is under investigation."

"My source says they are in for the high jump," that's all I know."

Are you sure? "You can bet your life on it."

"Remember what I say you don't tell anyone."

Okay I will remember. "With luck you will be a free man soon."

I can't wait for the day,

When I saw the look on his face my heart misses a beat.

It looks like I took something away from him, there was envy written all over it.

Then he looks at me, with along steady gaze, and say.

"It looks like you was an innocence man after all."

You would not believe it, yesterday I felt like hanging myself, thinking when is this going to end.

He sat very quiet staring into space.

That's when I decide to say thank you, and move away as quick as possible, because it seems the right thing to do.

"Hold on he said." Why I said? "What do you think about the news?" Well at least something happing out there I said.

"It's more than a start, they will have to look into your case again, but knowing the law they won't hurry."

"So keep your mouth shut, just sit tight he said."

That night I could not sleep, all I could think of is when I will get out, and what I can do for a living.

I have nothing; I will have to start all over again, but it will be better than been in here.

Then revenge came into my mind, I am going to sue them; at least I'll get some money to sort out my life again.

This was the longest night of my life, I though the night would never end.

How did the 'Boss, get that information about big foot 'Gurney,' and 'Lisa didn't? Why is she holding out on me? Is she doing her job? I have to talk to someone; if I don't talk to someone soon, I am going to blow my brain out the top of my skull just thinking.

With daylight, all the barriers I was putting up fell down.

I no longer feel the need to talk to anyone,' I am sure 'Lisa is doing her job, if I have to trust someone, I can think of none better.

On my way to breakfast 'Jerry, grabs my arm; 'Jerry, hold on don't ever grab me.

I don't like people grabbing me. "Jim, I am sorry."

"Do you want to know something he said?" Is it good? "I don't know."

So why tell me if you don't know? "Thought you would like to know they took 'Stan, away this morning in hand cuffs,' they took him very early."

How do you know this? "I saw them." What time? "About four thirty this morning I guess, I don't have a watch."

'Jerry, you were locked in. "Yea, but they had to walk pass my cell, so I took a quick peep."

I wander why they took him away? "Jim, they are afraid you will get to him and do a job on him, Ron said."

I don't think so.

'Ron, tell me something how long have you known me? "Over two year and six months I reckon."

Well you know how up standing a fellow I am, and how nice a person I am,' let's be honest, do you really I think I would do anything like that to poor 'Stan.

"Jim, do you want an honest answer?" Yes please. "Well I think you would add a little more to it, and just to prove that I am not bias, I would do the same if I had the nerve."

Well I must say this 'Ron, you are an honest person, you can tell the truth. "Jim, I glad the both of you think it's funny; I would hate to loose my balls 'Jerry, said."

Jerry, you have no use for them,' so there is no need for you to worry.' I only castrate people, who hurt me so as long as you don't cross me, your balls are safe.

'Ha, well 'Ron, said, we better stay away from 'Jim, you must not hurt him, or he will enjoy cracking your nuts."
'Ron, you better shut up or I'll do a special job on you for free.
'Jim, you are very kind, but no thanks, I have plans for my balls, why not do your own."
'Jim. Yes Jerry. "Here is a good idea, for you why not polish yours so when you are ready to use them they will be nice and shinny.

"Jim Jerry is right, you said you don't have a girl friend, so polishing them is a very good idea, don't you think, so when you get out they should be ready, if they are not, well the best tip I can give you is get rid of them, and send for me.
"Then you can crack your own nuts, because they are no good, and tell me when you are going to do it so I can come and watch."
'Ron, why don't you shut up, you are getting as bad as 'Jerry.' 'Jerry, you are spending two much time with him, he is picking up your bad habit he can't shut up.
'Jim, I will shut up after I say this,' "when I get out I will find you a very nice woman who will appreciate your slightly used well polish balls."

'Ron, you know what I like about you, you have so many good ideas that don't work.
"Jim, how do you know they don't work, you have not tried them?"
Ron, do you know you have a problem? "Yea I know I love women and money, you told me."
Before I could answer he said. "I am going to the television room, just in case you start doing that special job on me."
That is a good idea I said and they both walk away with 'Jerry, talking as fast as he could as usual.

I went back to my cell, and get stuck in my books, my studies was going well again.
I am glad I fond something, that takes my mind away from the four walls, even though I still have my bad days.

But when I have bad days I do as 'Ron, told me; and it works very well most of the time.

As I lay there stuck in my books, on a subject I just could not work out.

'Ron came back, 'Jim, "Dee is coming tomorrow, this time you must meet her,"

"I told her about you, say will you come." 'Ron, I have bad news for you, they will not let me into the visitor's room, without a visitor coming to see me.

"She said she have something very important to tell me I wonder what it is."

You see you don't need me there do you, she wants to see you in private.

'Ha, well you will have to meet her out side, or at our wedding," 'Say you will." Okay I promise. "Are you sure?" Yes I promise, I told you before if I am out I'll come.

Just then 'Jerry, walk in, with a big smile on his face. "Boy I have some good news for you 'Jim." "Man I have some good news for you."

I look up at him, come on spill it will you, since it's that good.

Don't just stand there and hope I can read your mind, spit it out.

"Detective 'Gurney, and detective, 'Bradford, they suspended them from duty this morning, pending the investigation into beating detainees, to extract confession."

What did you say? "I said 'Gurney." He starts to say it again, I heard you."

Stan must have spilt the beans. "Yea he did." I know I reply. "How did you know?" Never mind how I knew. "He told them that 'Gurney, told 'Brian, to rape you, and beat the crap out of you, short of killing you."

He promises Brian he would help him when he got out, but they did not say what kind of help.

Where did you hear this? "It was on the news."

Man that's good news; I am getting somewhere at last, good old 'Stan.'

"Wait there is more; I did not hear all of this because all the inmates start talking loud about your case when they heard the news.

"I am sure they say the police pick up a guy last night with a machete in his car and they are holding him for questioning." "That's' all I heard."

Next morning on my way for breakfast, the 'Boss's men stop me.

'The 'Boss, want to see you after breakfast in the yard 'okay." Ok, yea, tell him I will be there.

Again 'Ron said watch him 'Jim, he is a sly old bastard." I know 'Ron, I know you tell me, every time they come for me. "I just want to make sure you don't forget."

"Jim, it looks like you will be out of here before me, remember your promise to come to our wedding."

'Ron, for the hum teen time yes I'll be there, but don't you think you should ask 'Dee, first? "I told her about you already." Did you ask her if she will marry you? "No not yet." So how the hell do you know she will marry you? "Jim she will I know she will."

'Ron, I have no address, I have no where to live how are you going to find me? 'That is no problem; I will give you a list of address of people, and their phone number, they will help you," all you have to do is say I sent you, and tell them to call me," they all owe me a favour.

I will call you here; as soon as I find somewhere to live, and give you my phone number, so if she says she will marry you I will come, so will that stop you nagging me.

I took my time having breakfast, and slowly made my way to see the 'Boss, sit here please; he said, somehow that did not sound like him saying please, but I sat close enough to him, so I could hear him because as usual he was speaking very quiet he seems even quieter this time.

"Have you heard the news?" No but I was told. "Well here is a little bit more that is not on the news yet."

"They pick up a guy with a machete in his car, it's covered in blood, plus there was a lot of blood on this guy's clothes."

"He is been held for questioning."

I heard they pick up a guy, that was on the last night news, they did not say anything about him been covered in blood.

"This is not on the news yet; they suspect its human blood, they are waiting for the DNA result now."

"The police stop him for driving with one tail light; when they stop him he was acting strange so they took him in and search his car."

"They also found other items in the car, they call suspicious items but they did not say what it was."

"If I hear anymore I'll let you know." Thanks Boss.

"Again he repeat, remember I did not tell you this." Thank you, I'll remember, and I start to move away.

"Hold on just a minute please; I would like you to do me a favour."
Here we go ran throw my mind, payback time.

I look at him, surprise,' 'Boss, do you remember what I said when we
first met? "Yes we, you said no strings attach."

"I respect you for that, but things have changed."

I don't think so 'Boss, things may change for you but not for me.

"Jim I would not ask you to do this if I could ask someone else," it's
very important.

Hold on 'Boss, let me explain, I do not want to end up back in here,
so if you don't mind, I won't get involve in anything illegal, so count me
out.

I will not deliver, or carry anything for you; I have better things to do
with my life once I am out.

Not only that I am going to sue, for wrongful arrest, I am going to
make sure I never come back in here, so I will have to remain squeaky clean.
I start to leave again.

"Hold on please, here me first before you go, no one will be able to
trace anything back to you."

'Boss, if you don't mind, I still don't want to know.

'Jim, all I want you to do is phone a number I give you, and say Kim
123-789, and hang up.' Who can trace that back to you?" Mind you the
numbers I just told you is not the right numbers."

"I will give you the right ones just before you leave." I pause for quite
a while.

'Boss, I said, and I pause to think again, I still don't want to get involve
but I will think it over.

All he did while waiting for my answer, was stare into space.

When I finally look at him and say 'Boss, my answer is still no, weather
it can be traced are not.

He sat quiet, "and then he said, its okay don't worry about it."

"Okay but if you change your mind, there are a thousand big ones in it
for you."

'Boss, you know when I leave here I have nothing, and the police knows
I have nothing.

If I walk out with a thousand big ones, right away my goose is cook,
they will try to link that money to the shop or to you, and they will ask a lot
of questions, a whole lot of questions, like where I got it from.

111

They will trace it right back to you, because they know I spend a lot of time with you, and I will be back in here without my fucking feet touching the ground.

Hell 'Boss, I don't know how you can stand it in here, I don't know how long they are going to keep you lock up, but I will tell you this; if they tell me I have to spend one more year in here, I will run as fast as I can and ram my head in the wall.

I will hit the wall so hard; it should split my skull wide open like a coconut, but if for some strange reason I am freak of nature, and have a skull so hard it did not crack, it won't matter, because I am sure I will end up a dribbling brainless cabbage for the rest of my life, and that means someone will have to feed me with a spoon, and wipe my ass as long as I live.

"You are a fucking hard case aunt you?" 'Boss, I am going to ask you please don't let us go down that path, because it is not going to do either of us any good.

We sat in silence for a while once again looking into space.

'Boss, let me put it this way, if they find out I got the money from you, they will want to know why you give it to me, and I will tell them, because if I don't tell them they will drill me a new asshole that's for sure.

"Nut cracker what do you know about me?" 'Boss, nothing and to be honest, I don't want to know anymore than what I know now, and that is zero.

"So if you know nothing why do you think I am into something shady?" 'Boss, I don't think they put you in here for going to church.

Am I right or wrong? He looked at me very serious but said nothing.

'Boss, to be honest I don't care if what you are asking me to do is legal or not, I do not want to get involve if you don't mind.

Once again he look straight a head for a long time and then back at me.

It was as if he was looking straight through me, he made me feel like this was the end.

As I look down at his hands I thought any moment he would snap his fingers and his cronies would be all over me.

But instead he rubs his eyes, then his mouth, and his chin, with both his hands over his mouth he took a deep breath, look to his right and then to his left, then he shook his head as if to say I can't believe what I am hearing, this son of a bitch is saying no to me.

After a long pause he spoke, but from the sound of his, voice I could tell he was not pleased.

Then he said "okay I did not ask you to help me, no strings attach okay."

From the look on his face I knew that was not the end, and for the third time in my life I did not feel safe.

Then he said very quiet, so quiet I could hardly hear him.

If you need any help outside I can give you a number to call.

Thank you I said I will be alright.

Then as an after thought, I ask what kind of help? "You know a job what ever."

There will be no strings attach I promise he said quickly. Okay Boss I will remember your offer.

I had the feeling he was still trying to get a hold on me, he still want to get his hook into me even when I was free.

'Boss, I am sorry I have to turn you down, job wise. "Why?" Because I don't know what I will be doing yet, and whatever it is I will be taking my time, but thank you for your offer I said and walk away.

I could see from his face as I move away he did not like me saying no to him, once again.

But there was nothing he could do to get me to change my mind, and I think he knew it.

As I walk into my cell, and sit down a guard came in, "the warden wants to see you now."

You want to know something I said to the guard smiling; I don't want to see him.

"Should I tell him?" You know that could be funny I said, the trouble is, I won't be there to see his face when you tell him, so let's go and see what he wants. What you are waiting for I said as I push pass him into the passage.

I thought this is strange he only send one guard for me; there were "always" two with hand cuffs at the ready.

"Wait here he knocks on the door, and walk in, leaving the door half open, he said I have 'Jim, outside sir without hand cuff, should I put them on sir? "No, it's Okay 'Ray, he said."

"Tell him to wait in the waiting room."

Should I wait with him sir? "No that will be all, and 'Ray, please closes the door."

113

After a while the warden, open the door come in 'Jim, he said like we were long lost buddies.

"Have you heard the news?" Yes sir, I was told, this morning, I did not see it myself.

"It's looking good for you son." Yes sir.

"So what is your plan when you leave here?" I have none sir.

"Jim, I am going to be honest with you, I had this funny feeling from the first time I saw you; you did not look the type to break into a shop."

"This is detective 'Freeman, 'Jim, we are going to ask you to help us."

'Jim, there is a certain inmate you know well, he is always sending for you," we have a feeling he may ask you to do something for him." He paused for a few seconds.

"If he does will you tell us what it is?" I stood and look at him with disbelief; I just stood there as if frozen in time.

Then I look at detective 'Freeman, he was smartly dress with greying hair, and his shoes squeaky clean.

He sat with his legs cross looking at me as if I am there for him to use, and throw out when he feels like it.

But he said nothing.

I, look him straight in his blue eyes, my answer to you both is no I will not.

I will not help you or him, I am going to walk out of here and wash all the shit off, that I got stuck on me in this place, and believe me that will take a long time, because I can wash my hands and my body, but not my fucking brain.

'Son detective 'Freeman, said standing up.

Stop sir; with all due respect, I am not your son, nor the warden's, I owe no one in here or out there anything.

Sir if the inmate in question, who you are so worried about, wants to push a fire cracker up some ones ass and light it, it's all right with me as long as it is not my ass.

I will not be a carrier pigeon for you or anyone.

This discussion is over, I have no more to say, on the subject.

"We can still make things difficult for you detective 'Freeman, said."

What the hell can you do that is worse than what other people done to me already? In the past two years and nine months, everything that you can imagine some one did it to me.

One thing for sure you won't be the first to screw me, because some-one else beat you to it, so you hear me and hear me fucking good, don't make me fucking mad, because when I get mad I don't care a shit what I do, or what you do, so go on help yourself piss me off.

"And what do you think you can do in lock-up?" Well for a start I can kick up so much stink in here, that every prisoner leaving here, will have something to tell the news papers.

So don't threaten me anymore, if you know what's good for you, because I don't care a shit any more.

"Don't you threaten me he said?" You must have respect for the law.

I heard that one before, do you mean the one who screw up my life? Detective 'Freeman move closer to me, and I move closer to the door.

When he saw this he stops, and look at the warden then at me again.

"We must obey the law he said again."

By this time I was getting ready to start slinging some punches, so I said what fucking law, the one you people can twist to suit your self.

Why the hell are you using the law to threaten me to do something for you? And worse of all why should I obey the law.

I am in here for something I did not do, nearly three years of my life in this blasted cage.

He stood staring at me, for at least two minutes.

I know right about now, you feel like kicking the shit out of me "does-n't" you I said.

I know I am a very annoying person, so come on tell me what you want me to do, so I can tell you to fuck off, or go and tell the Boss what you are asking me to do.

Come on tell me please? Do you want me to jump up and down and say, thank you sir for locking me up? Or be a scared pissing creep for you.

Come on you tell me what I do, after I tell you what he asks me to do, and when he finds out I told you.

Will you be there to help me, when he stuck the fire cracker up my ass? I am sure you won't care a shit how wide he makes my ass.

Come on tell me what happens to me, once you get what you want.

Also when I leave here you know I will be forever looking over my shoulder, because his cronies will take pleasure in cutting my nuts off, and more.

You see if I become careless, I will be the one with the fire cracker up my ass.

Warden may I leave now before I do something I don't want to do? "Yes go."

I walk out the door, and pause in the passage, shaking my head and trembling, thinking once again I am in a corner.

What, do that son of a bitch's think I am? They cover me in shit up to my nose, now they want to bury me in it; I walk into the cell, still steaming mad.

You are having a very busy day 'Ron, commented.

Yea I said.

But he kept looking at me, as if to say are you going to tell me what it is all about.

'Ron, I am sorry my hands are tied; I cannot tell you anymore.

Maybe one day on the out side, in here the less you know the better off you, are remember you told me once.

He pauses for a while, and then starts to tell me about 'Dee, "coming," I am getting very nervous waiting for her, I feel so unsure; I never feel like this before.'

"Jim, it scares me, I can't sleep at night, and I don't even feel like eating these days."

'Ron, maybe that's what love does to you.

"Jim, I can't wait to get out of here, and make it up to her."

Hell don't tell me how you feel; tell her when you see her.

'Ron, at least you have something to look forward to. "Yes that's true." Sitting there chatting to 'Ron, a guard handed me a letter. "Nice perfume he said," it's from my lawyer? "I seen her, she is a nice bit of crackling, man she looks like a movie star not a lawyer he said, and walk away.

"Jim, I am very sorry I can't come to see you," I am up to my neck in work; two of our staff is off sick with the flue." The letter said.

"I would like to explain a few things to you, but I can't in a letter as you know," but rest a sure I have everything in hand; I promise I will explain when we meet.

"Best regards'

Lisa."

I was disappointed with her, everything is happing and she said nothing,
I "don't" think she would lie to me, I have to trust somebody.
While I was reading 'Ron, said nothing, he sat there looking at me.
It's my lawyer; she is lumbered with a lot of work.
I did not explain any more.

The rest of the day went by without anymore excitement, but the next
day all my wishes and hope came true, but with a bit of a "disappointment."

I was hoping this would never happen; when the 'Boss's, cronies came
for me they grab me by my arm and pull me, with no respect.

"The 'Boss, wants you now.' I stop I shout take your bloody hands off
me the both of you now, before I get mad.
All the other inmates stop and look at them.

Two guards came running over, and they let me go and walk away, but
the expression on their face was plain to see they were not pleased with me.
I ran after them now you go back and tell him I will come when I feel
like it, and tell him you grab me, and that's the reason why he is waiting.
I went into the yard the next day and I head straight for him.
His cronies saw me and came straight for me.
We all stop eye ball to eye ball, but they kept their hands to themselves.

For the first time I really look at them, and I was scared, I was only
eleven stone eight pounds.
Both, of them together were over thirty stones give or take a few
pounds, with muscles on their arms as big as my legs.
I look them in the eye for a long time, and at the same time looking
between them.
I could see the 'Boss, but I did not move.
Then a third crony came over, I never saw him before.
Let him go he said, and they step aside.
Then one said we will meet again, I stop and look at him I hope we do,
how about one on one I said.
He said nothing.

Even though I was scared I did not show it, because once again I reach
the point where I did not care.
I slowly walk over to the 'Boss, as I got close to him he said stop.
"Are you clean he asks?" Meaning, do I have a weapon.

117

Hell what do I need a weapon for? I am not mad at you, I am mad at your fucking cronies, for man handling me, no body threats me like a rag doll.

"You sure like to live dangerous don't you?" You are lucky; they did not break you in half and bring you to me."

'Boss, I told you before I don't care. So if that's the way it's going to be I don't think I want to see you any more; I "don't" need you, I thank you for your help with 'Stan, what more do you want.

Everything you tell me, I hear the next day from someone else anyway.

So what difference does it makes if some one tells me today or tomorrow? One thing for sure, I don't need you and the warden to mess up my life.

"What about the warden?" Suddenly I knew I should not have mentioned the warden.

"What about the warden he asks again?" If you must know he wants the same thing you want.

"And what is that?" He wants me to be a carrier pigeon for him, and detective 'Freeman. "Did you say Freeman?" Yes Freeman.

"So that son of a bitch is still after my blood, he is hoping I will make a mistake."

I could see from the expression on his face he did not like what I said, but I was in no mood to take any nonsense from him or anyone.

Or maybe because I said 'Freeman, that's why he ease off.

I start to walk away, "well before you go; here is a bit of news for you,' the machete they found in the car is covered with human blood.' They also found Mr. and Mrs. Jenkins hack to death in their home above the shop," after a neighbour told the police, that Mr. and Mrs Jenkins did not open their shop on Monday and Tuesday."

He starts reading the news paper.

The headlines said old couple hack to death in their shop,' Mr. Jenkins found at the bottom of the stairs in a pool of blood, and Mrs. Jenkins was found dead in bed."

He, stop reading and start telling what the paper said.

"The police said Mr, Jenkins, was fond lying in a pool of blood at the bottom the stairs, with his right arm completely severed."

"There was a flash light still in his hand on the floor, it was still switch on."

He also had a deep wound on the left side of his head just above his ear, almost splitting his skull in half.'

"Up stairs Mrs. Jenkins was still in bed, with her skull split in half."

"She was chopped in the centre of her head, detective 'Roland Lawson, said, she was facing her attracter lying down," we believe she was still a sleep when he chop her, splitting her skull almost down to her nose, from the side.

Detective 'Roland Lawson, "describe" the murder scene as gruesome; he would not give anymore details.'

Chief inspector 'William Darrin, also describe the science.

"Said it's the worst crime science, he has ever seen in thirty-five years in the forces."

"But he would not give any details."

"The killer did not give them a chance, 'Mr Jenkins' must have seen his face, or it was someone he knew."

"What we can't understand is why he went down stairs using a flash light instead of switching on the lights, he said."

'He would not give anymore further details, because there is an on going investigation.'

"He was asked if the man held in custody was responsible." 'It's two soon to tell, he said."

Chief inspector, Mr. and 'Mrs Jenkins, was rob two year and nine months ago,' is it possible this man is responsible for that crime; "we will be looking into that, and any other robberies done around that time," again it is two soon to tell."

Chief inspector if he did any of those robberies, that means there is an innocence man in prison? "Sorry I can't comment on that he said."

Five weeks later waiting in my cell, head down reading a voice said the warden wants to see you now.

As I walk into his office, sit down please he said.

Right away I knew something has changed, he never asks me to sit before or say please.

"I have some good news for you," we have someone in custody; he said he broke into the shop; they put you down for, two years and eleven months ago."

"The person that is been held gave this statement," he said the stupid

119

old man can't tell one black man from another," even thought I painted my face black.'

"If he handed over the money, the stupid old fool would be still alive."
Warden you said he painted his face black? "Yes that's what he said."

"You would not believe it; the stupid old fool grabs me," I had no choice, so I let him have it, because he would not let go.
"He confesses to both crimes, and others."

"I would like to be the first to apologize for what happen to you." Can I walk out right now? "No we are waiting for some papers from the courts."
He kept talking but I took no notice, I was in no mood to hear anymore from him, so I walk out of his office, without saying anything, or told to leave.

When I got back to the cell, 'Ron was like a cat with its tail on fire.
He jumps up as soon as he saw me, "Jim, you would not believe who I just saw,' have a guess." You saw 'Dee.
"Yes how did you know?" You told me. "Did I?" Yes.
"Oh, and somebody else came with her, have a guess who."
Come on 'Ron, I don't know who. "My son he said," she was pregnant when they put me down, she did not tell me."
"She said she really want to see that I change, before she could let me back into there lives." That is one sensible woman.

"Jim, who's side are you on?" 'Dee's, because if you go back the way you was, she is better off without you.
"Do you want to know something 'Jim?" You don't mince your words do you?" Why should I it is truth.

She is better off without you, if you are going back to chasing skirts, just imagine if you go out one night and pick up Aids, and take it back to her,' that's three lives fuck up, am I right? "Yes you are Jim."
So think about that next time you lift up a strange skirt.
I bet you never stop to think, you could take some kind of disease home to her, playing around like you do.

"You don't mince your words do you 'Jim, he said again? Why the hell should I, you ask me what I think, and I give you my answer as I see it.
'Ron, how many times have she been to see you now? "About five times maybe six."

Well she must have checked you out, and is satisfied that she can give you a second chance, that's why she told you about the kid now.

"That's true 'Jim, I never thought of it like that, thanks."

'Ron, do you want to here my news.

He was so wrap up looking at the photos he did not hear me; instead he got up and show me the photos, over and over again.

He stood close to me and watches me as I look at ever photo, remarking over and over look at him aren't he something, and aren't he is just like his dad.' He is a nice looking lad I said, but he is a lot better looking than you.

He smiles with pride, after he puts the photos away; I said do you want to hear my news now? "What news he ask?" "Yes please 'Jim."

"I am sorry I was so busy thinking of myself, I forget you went to see the warden today."

I am free; I could be out of here tomorrow, if the courts send the papers.

"What did you say?" You heard me.

He jump up in the air so fast several times shouting 'Jim's, free, 'Jim's, free, he was so happy anyone would think he was the one they was going to set free.

Then he sat down.

"Jim, that's marvellous news," you would not believe it, if someone told you we would both, have some good news for a change, would you."

"I bet you are happy?" 'Ron, I am scared, it may not come true; I am scared to go out those gates, I don't have anything out there; I 'don't' have a good suit any more.

"Jim you have nothing in here either do you, so you are only swapping nothing for nothing."

"What's the difference?" Look at it like this, outside you are free, you to go where you want, and when you want," and you still have time to make a life for yourself.

'Jim, you listen to me, go out there and kick ass."

"Shit man, take the rags of life and ring it dry,' carve your own groove, and don't look back."

"At least you will be free to make your own mistake." 'Thank s 'Ron.'

As I lay on my bed the night seems so long,' I remember another long night, just like this one, but somehow this one seems a lot longer and different.

This time I was waiting to walk out the gates, not thinking how to kill myself.

It was a relief to hear the guard open the door, and said have your breakfast first. Please tell me or someone when you finish."

Why? "I have to take you to see the warden as soon as you are finish, he is expecting you."

I did not feel like eating but I drank a few cups of "coffee," and chat with 'Ron, and 'Jerry, to pass the time away.

"Jerry asks what it feels like knowing you will be free in just a moment.

The only answer I could find, is Jerry you should know you done it so many times.

The news got around and all the inmates were very happy for me, because they know I was arrested for something I did not do.

I told a guard the warden want to see me; he took me to his office, he was busy on the phone.

But his secretary told me to come in and sit down, while the guard stood waiting.

When he hangs up the phone he came to the door, 'come in and sit down please.

I said no thank you, I prefer to stand.

He said you are still angry, and handed me an envelope, and said you are free; I took it and start to cry and walk towards the door, without saying thanks.

"Hold on please he said."

I stop and he starts to lecture me. "Hold on warden, I "don't" have to listen to any of your crap; I have to straighten out my life my way.

"You don't have to listen to what I have to say I know, but I am going to say it anyway."

"I know you are angry," I can understand that, but you can't jump on everyone who wants to give you some advice or help,' can you."

"Here is my advice to you, drop all the anger when you walk out the gates, because if you don't, you will be like all the other stupid fools who keep coming back here, they did not learn anything from been in here."

"Go out there and castrate somebody for pushing you around, you will be right back in here," you will not believe me I would hate to see that."

"Mistakes have been made and no one can change it, but you will have to find a way to live it."

Last but not least when your case comes up with 'Brian Manley, and 'Lonny Smith, I will be on your side, if I am needed, that is the least I can do."

"Also if there is anything I can do to help please let me know, give me a ring me here."

Warden I don't have time for you, the quicker I get out of here the better I will feel.

"He looks at me and the only thing he could find to say is you are angry aren't you?" You are darn right I am.

I walk out of his office without saying goodbye, or look back.

But his last words were "I will still be on your side when your case comes up."

When I went back to the cell 'Ron, pack all my books for me, he grab me gave me a hug.

"Go now before they change their minds, go and kick some butts and "don't" look back.

I must go into the yard before I leave. "What the hell for?" I am going to see the 'Boss.

"Why 'Jim, what the hell for why do you want to do that?" 'Ron, I am going to close a door once and for all.

"Jim, I hope you know what you are doing."

Ron I think so, I know I must do this to make sure the 'Boss, knows where I stand, 'Ron, if I walk away and don't say anything to him, he could get some of his cronies to come after me outside, and that's the last thing I need.

So I am going to close the door while I am in here, I am going to let him know I can't be a carrier pigeon for him.

"Jim, I told you he would want you to do something for him, I told you he would try and rope you in, why the hell you didn't stay away from the slime bag?" 'Ron something's is easier said and done.

Once I explain to him what is happening, I'll walk out, and I am sure he won't want me anymore, not even to clean his shit house, because he will feel he can't trust me.

"Man I hope for your sake you are right."

As I walk into the yard I could see the 'Boss, sitting in his usual place, when he saw me coming, he nods to his cronies its "okay."

123

I sat down beside him, "so you are free?" Yes.

"When will you go?" I am leaving now, I have my papers already.

I am here to thank you for helping me getting 'Stan, but I also have something to tell you before I go. We are been watched.

"I know I was tip off, after you leave me the last time."

"You are free to go, there are no strings attached.' Thank you.

'Boss, I would hate to leave here and keep looking over my shoulders.

"Why he ask, have some one been talking about me?" No, I just have this feeling about you; I feel you are a man that doesn't like any loose ends.

"So do you think you are a loose end?" No, but I am making sure you understand, what I will do and what I wont do no matter what.

"Jim, that's what I like about you."

'Boss, I'll say it again don't like me.

"There is nothing more to say then, so good bye and good luck." Bye 'Boss, and all the best.

At the front office they gave, me my old clothes and an envelope, I change my clothes; I was surprise they still fit.

They smelt a bit mouldy, but I had to wear them.

I walk to the gates and watch them open; it was as if a breath of fresh air rushes into my lungs, and it got fresher with every step I made, when I finally step through them, I wait to hear them close behind me.

Just, like I did, when they brought me in three years ago.

I stood there so nervous; I could just about hear them close.

Once again I was free, I stood there and look up at the sky, and then up the street and down the street wondering where to go.

Its mid November once again it was cold, dark and rainy.

I had nothing when I went in, and they give me nothing, not even a warm coat.

As I look at the sky, I whisper to my self here you are alone, with nothing but a few books, a buss pass and a few pounds in your pocket, what the hell you are going to do now 'Jim boy.

Hello 'Jim, my name is 'Ben Slater, I am from the daily, he start to say.

Get lost I don't want anything to do with you lot, he looks at me "surprise" as if to say what I have done to you.

None of you had anything nice to say about me, three years ago, you all found me guilty before the trial, so piss off.

'Tell your story now." I said piss off. "You need to say something."
Here is my story fuck off, if piss off is not clear enough.

And if you see any of the other garbage writers, tell them what my story is, so there will be no need for them to come looking for me either.

"Don't" you think if you tell your story now, you will be better off?" You don't hear so good do you? Do you want me to write it on your note pad? "No." Good bye then.

Then I heard another voice, said in broken "English" hello 'Mr. Jim, are you 'Mr. Jim?" Yea I am, what the hell you want, I snap.

"I was told to give you this letter and parcel, and to take you to wherever you want to go."

Who gave it to you I snap? "A lady gave it to me 'Mr Jim." Did she say her name? "No sir."

I stood and look at him for a while, thinking the 'Boss, set me up, then he said 'I am a taxi driver, 'Mr Jim."

"The lady is very pretty 'Mr Jim,' she told me where to meet you here, and what time to come," she said you will know who, when you smell the letter," that's all I know, so are you going to take the letter."

I took the letter as I open it I could smelt her perfume, and there was a key inside the letter.

It was from 'Lisa. Sorry I could not come to pick you up it said."

"I'll be in court when you walk out the gates, please tell the driver to take you to my address the address on top of this letter, I assume you won't mind."

"Love you, see you later."

'PS, please do not open the little parcel until you are in the house."

"I know you will want to open it; but I beg you please do as I ask."

'Jim, sir I was told you will tell me where to take you."

Yea number eleven, Stirling Street Brook Avon.

Do you know where that is? "Yes."

I took the parcel and step into the taxi, and start reading the letter again.

Then look at the parcel and smell it, her perfume was on it.

I read the letter again, and again, trying to read between the lines, to see if I could make some sense of it.

Looking out the window I feel like I was in a dream world by myself, thinking is this real.

Then from a far the taxi driver voice said. "We are here sir."

Thank you. "I reach into my pocket that's all right sir, the lady took care of it."

'Thank you I said again.'

I walk into the house, it was nice and worm, but I felt out of place.

In side it was a different world to mine, something, I have only seen in magazines.

I felt like I walk into its pages.

When I look around, nothing was out of place.

Then suddenly I get this feeling I have no right to be in here, even though she gave me the key.

I could smell the faint smell of her "perfume."

If it was not for that, I would be running away so fast, not even the wind could catch me.

Instead I sit on the edge of the settee with my parcel on my lap, ready to run for my life.

Thinking any moment I will be "arrested" for breaking and entering.

When the door bell rang I jump up shaking, but manage to calm myself down by the time I open the door.

The fellow at the door hand me a bag,' I could smell Chinese food.

Thank you, I reach into my pocket, it's "Okay" sir; the lady took care of it sir.

Thank you I said.

I place it on the dining table, and open it and sit down.

Then the phone rang, again I jump; up so fast I almost spill the food.

"Hello 'Jim, are you alright?" It's me Lisa." Yea, I am fine.

"You don't sound unsure, are you sure you are okay?" Yes I am fine now I here your voice.

"Jim, I am very sorry I could not meet you." That's okay.

Make yourself at home see you later. 'Oh' did they deliver the food?" Yea I got it.

"There is beer and wine in the fridge; if you want something stronger it's in the bar just helps your self." Thank you.

Bye she said and hangs up.

I sat down to eat again when I remember the parcel; I open it, in side another note.

'Jim, please open the little parcel," and again there was another little note.

'Jim, it say's these are the white ones, I was going to wear them today."

"For the first time in my life I have gone out the door without wearing one."

"When I get home you can put them on for me," or leave them off, it's up to you."

I had to walk around the sitting room several times before I could sit down.

Forgetting the Chinese food she bought me.

And again the phone rang.

"Jim, did you open the parcel?" Yes. "Do you remember the question you ask me three years ago," When you first met me?" Yes.

'Well the time has come for you to find out what it is like," that is if you are still interested."

"I hope I can live up to your expectation." I froze.

"Are you there 'Jim? You have gone quiet.' 'Lisa, I said and stop.

Then she said do you want to know something?" I never knew court rooms were that cold and draftee until now," my butt is cold, 'ha, well never mind, as long as yours is worm, she said laughing."

'Lisa, are you sure? 'Yes, I am sure my butt is cold."

You know I don't mean your butt.

"I know what you mean, but my butt is still cold."

"The answer to your question is yes, from the first day I saw you."

"Sorry I have to go now see you later bye."

'

"Oh, is the Chinese's food Okay?" I did not know what else to get?" Yes it's nice.

"Bye I have to go this time, bye."

There goes my dream again I said.

"No not this time 'Jim, not this time," it's going to be the longest day of my life."

"Sorry I must run I am due back in court, sorry I must to go," "Okay" Bye.

I ate a bit more and put the rest in the fridge.

Then took off my shoes and lay on the settee, suddenly all the stress was gone, and fall a sleep.

It seems I was asleep for only a few minutes, when I felt a cold hand on my face, and hear her soft calm voice saying is that all you have to do, as she kneels down on the floor,

She took my face in both her cold hands and kisses me on my forehead.

"I dreamt of this moment for three years, I know it is real now, but it is like a dream."

With her face so close to mine, for the first time I could feel the warmth of her breath on my face, it sends a tinge down my spine, as I reach up and holds her in my arms for the first time.

I whisper in her ears my dreams came through.

"Yes and mine she whisper back into my ear."

"I thought that would wake you up she said, cold hands and cold lips."

What else is cold I ask? "That will be telling she said." Please tell. "No I only tell over the phone."

"I'll get a shower to warm the cold bits," and then cook you some food; I have not eaten a lot today," I did not feel like food to be honest."

Why? I had my mind on other things she said.

What other things? "Jim, I'll tell you later."

Well is there anything I can do? "No not yet, later."

Yes later she repeats with her famous smile I got use to.

'Lisa, May I ask you a question.

'If it's the same question you ask before, the answer this time you will have to wait for it."

I got hold of her before she could get up.

"Jim, will you do me a favour; leave me to do my work first."

What work? I have to cook and have a shower; and I'll be in court again tomorrow, so I have a few things to prepare."

Can I wash your back "Oh no,"...." Oh no.... that is asking for trouble."

"And what would my mom say if she finds out?" I won't tell her if you "don't."

If you are in that much of a hurry to find out what it's like in heaven, you can help me in the kitchen, but keep your hands to your self."

'Lisa, you are wicked, treating me like this, my finger nails are falling out hanging on like this.

'Ouch that must hurt, would you like a cup of tea it may save your nails she said.

'Jim, ever since you said those words to me.

What words? "Think about it 'Jim, I know you haven't forgotten them."

"I will be honest with you, I been loosing more than my nails," I been living a life of torment, asking myself should I get involve with you; at one stage I thought I was going mad; I couldn't get you out my mind, you haunt me every night, and what made it worse, I could not say what I want to say to you when I see you."

"I suddenly got up one day and decide I am going to follow my heart no matter what," I decide I was going to live my life my way no matter what, and that's when I started to feel better.

"So come and help me in the kitchen, so we both can find out what haven is like."

What are you cooking? Give it to me I will do the cooking.

"Can you cook?" Well you have to wait and see I have not cooked for a long time; so it will be a new experience for me too.

I'll have a shower; can I wash your back? "The answer is still no."

'Jim, you have a one track mind." Who me? "Yes you."

"Can't you see there is no one else here?" Surprise me think about cooking and make it good."

She had a shower and lays the table, and brought me a glass of wine, hug me from behind.

That smells good she said.

No you smell a lot better I said.

She kisses me on the side of the neck again.

Go please you are in my way I said.

"So you don't want me now that I been in the shower." 'Lisa, what she said, as she turns around I hesitate."

"What she said?" Thank you for being here.

I had no idea where I was going when I walk out those gates, I felt like asking them to let me stay, even though I hated the place.

She came back and hugs me, and gave me a sip of her wine.

'Jim, if you did that I would come and drag you out by your ears, all the way home, then plea guilty for pulling your ears off."

"Well since you don't want me I will go and prepare some work for tomorrow while I am redundant."

I put the food and a bottle of wine on the table.

"She was sat at her disk, working that smells good she said again, if it taste half as good as it smells you can do the cooking from now on."

I don't think so.

"Why not, if it smells like this all the time?" I hate cocking that's why.

This is good, she ate and have second helping,' this is good, where did

129

you learn to cook like that?" Nowhere all I did is bang it all in and hope for the best.

It's only good because you did not eat today.

"No it is good."

I start to clear the table while she was still eating.

I took a dish of strawberry and ice in. "You will make me fat." I don't think so."

"I'll wash up she said." No I will.

"No you did the cooking, I'll wash up."

No, please go and do your work. "Thank you sir I will do that."

When I finish I sit on the settee. She was still working.

"After a while she said 'Jim, are you all right?" Yes I am why? "You are very quiet."

I am all right thanks.

"Are you always this quiet?" Yes Sometimes.

"You are not worrying about anything are you?" No.

Lisa it is so quiet here; I am use to a lot of noise and inmates shouting at each other.

"Put the TV on it won't bother me."

Are you sure? "Yes I won't be long."

"Can you pure me another drink please."

What would you like? "You choose."

I took her another glass of wine; place it in front of her, and I gently push her hair away from the back of her neck, and kiss her on the neck, she gasps for breath.

"Naughty, naughty, you are hitting below the belt."

That is the idea I said. "Now I don't feel like working anymore."

Sorry, I will sit over here until you are finish I promise, I won't interrupt you again even if you want another drink.

After a while she came and laid her head in my lap, and put her long legs upon the settee arms and the smell of her perfume slowly drift up my nose.

As I look down in her eyes, her dressing gown falls slowly off her legs.

My heart was beating so heard I could feel my chest going in and out.

'Jim, you want to know something your clothes smell mouldy, I know I am sorry; this is the only clothes I have.

"Its alright I know." My hands began to shake.

"Jim, it's okay, I am shaking also."

"She sat up and we kiss, 'hi, she said, let's go to bed."
I'll have a shower first, I smell of like mould plus the kitchen.
"Don't be long, I'll get some drinks."
"Have you been up stairs yet?" No.

She picks a bottle and put some ice in a bucket. "Come I'll give you a tour, this is the bed room, and the bath room is in there, don't worry about the rest; you can see that tomorrow all by yourself, if you feel like it."

I walk into the bath room, and she came in with me; can I wash your back she whispers in my ear?" Yes, if I can wash yours.
Then she unbutton my shirt, and pull my belt, her hands was shaking, as my pants fell to the floor.
I pull her dressing gown tie, pushes it off her shoulders.
She reach into the pocket, took out something I did not see what it was.
She had nothing on under the dressing gown, in her hands the white knickers she gave me.
"Do you want to put these on now; she said smiling please do it now, before you get your self in trouble." What kind of trouble I ask? "I don't know but I thought I better give you a chance to change your mind before you go two far."

And I thought you were still cold? Well I'll put them on tomorrow morning before you go; to make sure your butt is worm from now on.
She drops them and we step into the shower.
"Jim, do you want to know something?" Yes what. "I am where I want to be for the first time in my life.
'Lisa, I am where I want to be also.
She did not wash my back; she started washing the parts we were waiting so long for. Then all have of a sudden she grab my tool and lead me out of the shower.
Grabbing two towels in the other hand, turn her head and gave me one of her haunting smile, that say here I am come and get me.

'Lisa, I have to go back in the shower, I am still cover in soap.
While finishing my shower, I thought I better hurry before she's changes her mind.
I got out of the shower as quick as I could grab a towel, dry my self and ran into the bed room.
She was lying on the bed still necked, arms out stretched waiting for me.
I pause for a moment, looking at what I waited so long for.

When I got on the bed she dive on top of me, held me so close I could hardly breathe.

I gently pushes her up and looks into my eyes, she said something, I did not hear.

I could feel her soft hands holding my tool.

From then on the joy of getting what I wait for so long was just as I thought it would be it was share heaven.

The rest is history; I just lay there not moving, saying nothing, when her voice brought me back to this world.

"Jim, are you alright?" Yes I whisper.

"Are you sure you are alright?" Yes I am why? I thought for "moment" I killed you."

I whisper what a way to go, remembering, what 'Ron, said for a brief moment.

"Then she laughs out loud."

What so funny I ask? "You dying on top of me, how would I get you off, how could I explain it?" Well you could tell them I was starving, and you gave it me and my heart could not take the strain.

"Very funny, if you get off me now, I will get something to drink."

No I am not finish yet I said smiling.

"Well lets have a break, and a drink, and you can do it again she said."

I got off, she ran into the bath room, after a while she came back, and pours some drinks.

I went to the bath room, when I came back she was under the covers.

She pushes the covers aside for me and gave me a glass of "champagne" this is nice I thought but said nothing.

We said nothing, as we sip the champagne, looking and touching each other.

'Lisa, be careful how you squeeze my tool I said.

"She starts laughing," what did you call it?" That's my tool. "Jim that is the first time I ever hear it call a tool."

"Why don't you call it your prick, or your cock, and if you want to be discreet call it your private."

No thank you, I still like to call it my tool.

'Lisa, yes, do you know what you are doing? "Yes I am in bed with the man I want to be in bed with squeezing his tool."

You know I don't mean that.

'Jim, 'I know what you are thinking," don't worry about it, we will cross that bridge when we comes to it, so if you are still worried about what other people will say, and the media 'don't, I am not."

Lisa I am worried about you telling your Mom and Dad, what are they going to say.
"I spoke to them a long time ago, I am sure they know how I feel about you."
'Let's enjoy the champagne, let's leave the world out side," she took my glass and fills it again.

I took a few sips, and put it on the night table, and we melt into each other arms and fell a sleep.
When I woke she was up and getting dress.
Here you are she said smiling as I open my eyes, you have a choice of colours which one would you like me to put on?' Red I said red for danger.
Today will be a long day I said.
"Why?" Because you know, what I will be thinking about all day.

"Jim, you are a dirty old man, thinking about that all day."
Here we go you got it wrong, what I mean I will be thinking about you.
But if I am thinking about that it's your fault I am thinking about it you planted the idea in my head.
"Go on blame me she said with her famous smile."
"What would you like to drink? Coffee please, she brought me a coffee and kisses me on my forehead.
"I will be home for 2:30 pm, sharp be ready, we are going shopping; she gave me a small kiss on the cheek again then hurry to the door.
At the door she stops.
You will find every thing you want for breakfasts in the cabinet, above the fridge, or in the fridge if you feel like cooking, have a good look and you will find what you want, 'bye.'

As I lay there drinking the coffee, and looking round her bed room, nothing was out of place, it was so neat and clean I thought for a moment, I woke up in a store show bed room, I did not notice it last night.
If it was not for the smell of her perfume, there is no way I could convince myself I was not still dreaming.
What does she want with me I ask myself? She's got everything, and I

133

have nothing; we live in two different worlds.

After a while I answer my own question, time will tell, all I can do is, go with the flow.

I got out of bed have a shower ate breakfast and made the bed, tidying up was easy
because nothing was out of place, away from in the bath room, that take me all but twenty-five minutes to clean.

I went down stares sit on the settee, got my books and start to work; the thought went thought my mind again, nothing is curtain in life, so I must study hard to achieve what I set out to do before I met her.

I can't depend on her to give me everything, like 'Ron, gets from his girl friend.

Even if she is rich I must make my own, I must make myself "independent" if I have my own no one can take it away from me; just then the phone rang and took me away from what I was thinking.

Are you alright? Yes"…" why? Just"…."just checking you are still there, I had to make sure I did not dream about last night.

Was your dream good? "That's my secret."
Come you can tell me. "No I can't tell secrets."
I will run a way if you don't tell me.

It is still my secret, she said again laughing. "What are you doing?" I am reading my books, and what are you doing? "I am on my way down to the court house."
"Don't forget I'll be home at 2:30." Okay. "Bye loves you."

It was so quiet in the house I find it a bit hard to settle down.
So I put the radio on very low, I find I could work better with some noise.
When I look at the clock it was 12: 30 pm I put down my books, and search for something to eat.

When the phone rang again, a voice said hello is that you 'Jim? Yes speaking.
'This is 'Lisa's, Mom, how are you?" I am fine.
"Lisa told me you were home."
She was in for a long chat; it was like she knew me all her life.
After a while she said hope to meet you soon, bye 'Jim.'

134

Okay Mom bye nice talking to you.

I ate and went back to my books.

When I hear the front door open I look up at the clock, it was 2:33 pm, after a while she came into the room, naked, I told you to get ready for 2:30 pm she said smiling.

'Shame on you, come ill get you ready, since you are two lazy to do it yourself ready,' I'll do it for you.' 'Stand up please, I did not hesitate, she knew what she wanted and took it.

"Jim, I had this feeling all day." Now you tell me.

So are you all right now? 'Yes, but it was not that.

"I had this feeling I would come home and you are not here, I don't know how I get through the day." Why? "Maybe it's because I really feel happy, for the first time in my life."

'Lisa, I am not going anywhere, firstly I wanted you for so long, why should I go now, and second I have nowhere to go, so you can forget the idea that I will run away.

'She got up; I thought I told you to get ready for 2:30, what are you doing naked? I told you that we are going shopping."

Why are you still naked? I don't know what I am going to do with you she said, as she ran up stairs laughing, and into the shower. I ran after her and got in with her.

Your, mom call, "I know she told me." She said you sound like you are a nice person."

She was in for a long chat. "That's Mom for you."

What did you tell her about me? "I told her everything about you I always tell my Mom everything."

You told her everything? "Yea I told her about you the first day I met you."

'So if you are not nice to me, I'll tell her what you did to me last night,' and what you done to me as soon as I get home from work today, tired and worn out.

"I'll tell her how you jump on me as soon as I walk through the door."

If you don't watch it I'll jump you again tonight.

"Is that a promise?" Come on lets get out of here before I jump you now. "You bad boy, what are you trying to do kill yourself, or you just trying to make up for lost time?" Ha, 'ha, very funny.

135

"Jim if you are not going to do it let's go shopping, so you can look smart when you meet my Mom and Dad."

When are we going? "We are going tomorrow morning;" sorry I should have told you."

On the way to her parent's home, she was very quiet.

'Jim, your case I'll have to turn it over to Daddy, or would you like to use someone else?"

What case? "We are not finished yet, you can sue for wrongful arrest, and everything that happen to you when you were in custody."

"Also the three inmates may have a case against you, and you against them."

"You have a case against detective 'Gurney, and 'Bradford, for slamming you against the wall." Now that it's proven they beat detainees.

"I can no longer represent you because I am involved with you; I will speak to Daddy as soon I get there." I'll ask him for his opinion and the best way to handle this."

"I will also ask him if he will take your case, if you don't mind, I know he will enjoy doing it."

That's okay with me; I'll leave it all to you, you what is best.

She went quiet again.

You're very quiet, are you afraid that you're parents wont like me? "No, I told them about you, from the first day I met you, remember."

'Jim, I told them everything, I don't hide anything from them," I have other things on my mind."

"Don't" worry if Daddy gets out the shot gun, and put it to your head."

'Ha, well I have been to heaven already so it's worth it.

"Well if daddy shoots you I will shoot him for taking away heaven from me."

After two and hours drive we turn up a very narrow country lane, then into a tree covered drive, set in between the trees a cottage, and a very large well maintained lawn.

As we pull up out side, her Mom and Dad came through an arch way, from what I assume was vegetable garden, because they were carrying vegetables in a small basket.

It was very cold when we got out the car.

Mom, Dad this is 'Jim, he wipe his hand down the side of his trousers before he shook mine, 'hi, 'Jim, hello sir, hello Mom, please to meet you, she gave me a peck on the cheek.

Come Mom said, lets get out of the cold, as she slip her hand through my arm, still carrying her little basket in her other hand.

We went to the back of the house, I open the door and she walk in.

Would you like a hot drink, or something stronger 'Jim, hot please mom, 'Tea?' That will be fine thank you Mom.

First look at 'Lisa's, Mom I could, see she is a very confident woman, and right away I find my self very relax, because she made me feel at home.

Looking at her face I could see where 'Lisa got her beauty from,' she must have been a cracker in her youth,' I thought.

She was almost the same height as 'Lisa, and still very slim.

I could understand why 'Mike, marry her.

I was not sure about him; confident is two mild a word to describe him.

He looks the type of person who is use to getting his own way.

Maybe he feels the same way about me.

But for now he accepts me, without asking any questions, however I have a sneaky feeling there will be a few questions later.

He too must have been a handsome fellow in his youth, I thought; with greying by his temple it made him look very distinguish, and been very slim and tall, I should think most people have to look up at him.

From the way he walk and talk, I could see he was the no nonsense type of person, in a way I think he is like me with a difference.

He uses the law to crush his victims, and I use my fist.

I look out the window 'Lisa and her father stood there talking, as if it was a nice summer's day.

"Don't take any notice of those two, her Mom said, they are always like that, chat, chat, chat, as soon as they meet," I don't know what they find to talk about half the time," they work at the same place, yet when they meet; it is as if they have not seen each other for months."

"Come sit she pull a chair from under the dining table for me, make your self at home."

She place four cups and saucer on the table, and a little plate with biscuits.

Nice to meet you at last she said, pulling out another chair and start to sit then stop as the kettle start to whistle. She pure the hot water in the tea pot,' then tap on the window, and beckon to 'Lisa, and her dad to come.

As Lisa walks in, she pulls out a chair and her dad sit down.

Her Mom pulls out a chair for 'Lisa, and she put her arm around my shoulder and kisses me on the cheek, and wipe off the lip stick with her cold fingers.

Then turn around and gave her Mom a hug.

Would, you like something to eat 'Jim? Dinner won't be long.

No thank you Mom, I am fine.

'Jim, yes sir I answer, please call me 'Mike.

'Lisa, just ask me to take your case, and she explain the reason why,' she told me that it's okay with you." Yes sir.

She gave me all the disks, and papers, if I need to know anymore I'll get in touch okay.' Yes 'Mike thanks.

We chat for a while; but he said nothing more about my case,' but deep down I have this feeling he wanted to ask me something about myself.

"Come I'll show you around before dinner 'Lisa, said, lets go out side first."

She was like a little child that was glad to be home.

Don't stay two long I'll get dinner soon. "Okay Mom."

Can 'Jim, borrow your Wellington Daddy? "Yes help yourself."

"I'll tell you now it's very muddy and slippery down the path, we had a lot of rain this week, so be careful he said."

She took my hand and lead me around the garden, and shows me the scenery, I could see for miles in the valley.

She pointed out the different things in the distant,' as we walk down a narrow muddy foot path, walking behind her, between the trees I said that is nice.

"What she ask?" Your butt is.

"Jim, again I know what you are thinking about," so you are a mind reader? "No she said."

Well this time you're wrong I said.

"Why am I?" Because its two cold and I don't like wet grass I answered.

"That is nice to know; now I know how to keep you off me."

Me off you that is funny, ha, ha, ha.

After a while we came out onto a nice lawn, with a lot of apple and pear trees in the garden at one side, and on the other side a very high hedge.

It was as if the people who plant the hedges, wanted to keep the beauty of the place a secret.

"This was my grandmother's home; this is where I was born,"

138

Grandmother gave it to me after daddy bought his house from my cousins, they had to sell it and share the money after there mother died.'

"My uncle was her husband, he died of war wounds I didn't know him."

"I love this place; I would love to bring up my kids here."

It's rented out at the moment, so we can't go inside, unless they invite us in.

It will need modernizing in side but not two much; I would hate to spoil the beauty, because it is very old,' it was built in the sixteen century."

"I rented it out because it needs someone living in it, they take very good care of it and the garden; that's part the agreement; I don't have time to look after it."

'Lisa, have you told your parents everything about me? "Yes and no."

What do you mean by yes and no? 'Jim, I told them from day one that I believe you were "innocence."

What did they say when you told them you was involve with me? "I told them nothing." 'Jim, I did not know until yesterday myself, so I could not tell them."

"But I told Mom over a year ago, how I felt about you."

So what did you tell her, when you know you was involve me? "Do you really want to know?" Yes I would like to know.

"Well I haven't said anything about the first night yet."

What about the first night? "Jim, don't tell me you forget already?" Forget what.

"You know what I mean." No I don't.

'Jim, you got out, and have your wicked way with me all night."

'Ha, 'ha' very funny, now I know what you were think about all the time, I was in side.

'Lisa, you are worse than I am.

If you really think about it, it was the other way around; you are the one who screw me.

"Come on 'Jim, who begs who like a little puppy the first time we meet?" 'Lisa, begging and doing is not the same.

"You were lock-up and if I had the nerve you would have me on the table," come on tell the truth."

Yes I would.

"Jim, listen please can I ask you a question?" Did you enjoy your first night out?" 'Lisa, can I do it again tonight, to make sure I was not dreaming."

"You are not inside anymore so there is no need to dream; do you know what your trouble is 'Jim, you are greedy." Me greedy I don't think so.

"I would love to do it again tonight but, I don't think mommy and daddy would like to hear you banging me all night."

Are we staying the night tonight? "Yes, I pack some of your new stuff so we can stop the weekend.

"Sorry 'Jim, I should have told you, is it okay?" Yes.

"I must stop that." Stop what? "Organising, people's lives, sometimes I swore my job is taking me over."

It's be nice to be with a happy family again, it's been so long, I forget what family life is like, so don't let it worry you.

By the time we got back to the house dinner was ready, I was very hungry when I sat down, and I really enjoy the meal.

'Mike did not say a lot, until we went into the sitting room. Taking a bottle of wine with him, he offers me a drink.

Then he asks what plans I have work wise.

I told him that I was taking a course in electrical engineering.

"Oh, yes 'Lisa said something about that," she also said you were good."

As soon as we get back, I'll be looking for a job, and continue with my studies.

"If I can help please don't be afraid to ask he said." 'Lisa heard him, as she walks in with the "coffee" help with what she ask?" "We were talking about work."

"What kind of work?" What 'Jim is going to do."

"Daddy he just got out after three years in lock up, he doesn't need to think about work yet," also he's got to go back to court, to make sure the people who mess his life up pay for it, and he may have to face possible charges, from those two fools in side."
'

"Jim, there is no need to hurry, have a rest let the government keep you for a while," she said."

"They kept you inside; let them keep you out side, It was not your fault why you lost your previous job, was it?" So take some time to decide what you would like to do to sort his life out."

I don't know if it's because 'Lisa, told 'Mike, I don't need to start looking for work yet, why he did not continue the discussion, or maybe it was too early, for him to think I am planning to live off her.

'Lisa went back into the kitchen, and returns with two more glass.

As she leave the room he said, "Jim, if I know 'Lisa she will be working overtime on your case even though she gave it to me."

"And she will be at my throat everyday from now on, to sort out the government for your compensation."

She came back just in time to hear most of what he was saying, so she just looks at him and said nothing.

He picks up some of the papers 'Lisa gave him, and starts to read, and at the same time he kept talking to me.

Then he went quiet, as if there was something he saw in Lisa's notes.

The next thing I heard was 'Lisa, and her mother laughing out very loud, in the kitchen.

Listen to those two 'Mike said; wish I knew what that was about.

Then 'Lisa and her mom join us, we sat talking for a long time; they did not ask me anything about prison life, I was very glad, because that was still a sore spot in my life I sooner forget.

While, sitting there every time I look at Mrs Myrna, she was looking at me; it was as if she was trying to decide if I am good enough for her daughter.

Mom, do you mind if 'Jim and I go out for a drink? "No go on enjoy yourself."

When we got out side she said, "I though you would love a break."

No I was fine you parents are very nice.

"Wait until daddy start grilling you, when I am not around, you will sing a different tune."

I am sure your Mom is grilling me right now; she did not take her eyes off me.

"I know I saw her, she told me in the kitchen she likes you."

Ha, well it's nice to know that the two women are on my side, so your dad doesn't stand a chance does he? "I don't know 'Jim, I am a daddy's girl."

What was your mother grilling you about in the kitchen? "She was not grilling me."

So why were you laughing so loud? "If you must know she asks me about you."

Ask what? "You know what."

No I don't know what.

"She wants to know if you were good in bed." You lie. "I don't lie."

"I told her you beg me for sex the first day you saw me."
"She could not understand, how you could be thinking about sex, at a time like that."

A time like what do you mean? "You know they were going to lock you up and you had sex on your mind."
You did not tell her, "Yes I did." You lie. "No I don't lie."
"I told her, and she though it was funny."

Oh, shit you really mean it don't you? "Of course I mean it."
"She is my mother and my best friend, we have no secrets."
I have to face her tomorrow.
"Jim, I told her from day one the first chance I get, I was going to bed with you."
"Well that nice to know, you told your mother but not me."
"There is no way I could tell you."

Why? "Well for starters you were in lock-up," what would you do if I told you, away from dream and pull out all your hair?" I would have thought of something.
"Like what? Cry all night long."
So you planed it all? "Of course I plan it, 'Jim I knew what I want," and I took it."
And there was I thinking I was the one in charge.

"I am sorry 'Jim, but it's your fault, you ask me first, all I did is give you what you ask for," are you sorry?" No because if you had left it to me, when I came out, I would not have the courage to ask you again."
I "didn't" even know where I could find you, yet alone ask you to go to bed.

When I walk out those gates, I had no where to go, so quoting my father's famous words, find some where to lay your head, before you find somewhere to put your tool.
So all I was thinking about is where was I going to sleep that night,' and how was I going to survive.
"So you mean to tell me you did not remember me?" Yes I did, but I ask myself why you would want with me? You never show your feeling.
"Jim, I am sorry I could not tell you, I thought understood."
At times I did, and sometimes I could see it in your eyes but when I was away from you, I was not sure you had any feeling for me.

142

"It's funny 'Jim, I knew how you felt about me; I could see it in your eyes every time we meet."

Going, back to you telling, your mother everything about me.
'Lisa, I will not go to bed with you again, if you are going to tell your Mom.
"Jim, you want to bet?" No. "You are a coward; I did not know you were a coward.
I know you don't have to tell me.
'Lisa, I know what you are trying to do, you want me to give you an excuse, to jump me. If I say I won't go to bed with you again, you will jump on me the first chance you get.
"You are a clever lad aren't you?" No just been careful, because if you get me in a corner you know I can't walk away.

"Why cant you?" Because you know a standing cock has no conscience."
"I use to think men were invincible, when it comes to sex."
You want to know something 'Lisa, I am, but I don't want to take advantage of you.
"Jim, I don't think you can take advantage of me."
'Lisa, I know somebody else just like you.' 'Who is he or she?" He is in prison.
"How is he like me?" He talks about sex and money all day.
"Jim, I don't just talk about it; I do it," do you want me to give up?" 'Oh, hell no that would break my heart.
"Well why you are complaining?" I am not complaining.
To be honest it's nice to know a woman, who knows what she wants, so just keep playing I am happy, but don't forget I been in lock-up for three year.

"I know that, you "don't" you have to tell me, that is why I am keeping you happy."
"I "don't" want you to say you are hungry, are look at me like you did every time I visit you in side."
"You made me feel guilty, when I visit you sometimes."

How did I do that? "Jim, you look so sorry for yourself, your tongue was hanging out," at times I feel like taking off my clothes, and "surrender" to you," because I felt the same."
'Lisa, I know this may sound funny, sometimes I have to pinch myself

now; because I just can't believe this is happening to me.

"What do you mean?" I mean I found someone who wants me for what I am, because I have nothing but me."

"Do you want to know something 'Jim, if it's any consolation I feel the same way?" For the first time in my life I feel complete."

I want you to know this 'Jim, everything I give to you I give with love, so don't feel embarrass to take it please."

When, we sat down to have our drink in the pub, a lot of regulars who knew 'Lisa came over to say hello.

They all look at me, and start to ask, are you they would ask?" 'Yes he is 'Lisa, would answer very quickly, but please, "don't" tell anybody.

"Okay they would say.

And then she would say, please don't ask anymore questions about him will you.

Then they would ask her how is the family was and leave, we were lucky most just ask her how long she will be staying.

"Jim, the trouble with country folks is everybody knows everybody," I was born here my parents was born here, and my grand parents."

"I don't need to say anymore do I?" No, no need.

'Hi, 'Lisa, 'hello 'Nick, how are you?" I am fine; 'Nick, this is 'Jim."
Hello 'Jim.

Hi I answered "Nick writes for the local papers."

I thought here we go, here comes the questions.

'Hi, he said again.

"Are, you he start to say."

Yes 'Jim Sears, I answered and again he starts to say you are,' and again I say 'Jim Sears.

'Jim, I heard you were out, every reporter in the country is looking for you to write your story." I don't have a story 'Nick.

"Surly there is something you would like to say in our local rag." 'Nick, I don't have a story.'

"Lisa, can I ask you this question?" What, was it like to loose your first case?" 'Lisa, look at me and look back at him but said nothing.

"Jim, you was a lucky man to have 'Lisa, in your corner, most of us feel 'Judge Wilson, put his foot down on 'Lisa, because she volunteered her services for free."

"We think 'Judge Wilson, think 'Lisa took your case for the publicity or to run hot rod over the court and get you off."

We think, he thinks a high power lawyer like 'Lisa, should not take cases like yours."

Nick, that's where you are all wrong, I volunteer my services when I heard about 'Jim's case on TV, but I am not prepare to say why I took it."

"I am sorry, let me put it a different way, when I heard the news, and read about it in the papers next day, I had this gut feeling this man was not guilty, "don't" ask me why," because I don't know, and that's when I volunteer my services for free, I hope that answer your question."

Now the whole world knows I was right, even though I did not win the case.

I hope I answer your question 'Nick?" 'Yes, but you sounds bitter.

You are right I am bitter, I don't like to loose when I know I am right, and because I was cheated a man spent three years in prison.

"Can I print that?" 'Yes 'Nick, as long as you don't add to it.

"Jim, are you going to tell me what it is like to be free?" Nick, I just said there is no story.

This is my first night out, so do you really want to know what its like to be free? "Yes."

Well go and get yourself lock up, and come out after three years, then I bet you won't ask that question.

"Jim, I am sorry I have to write something about this, it's not everyday I get to meet someone like you and 'Lisa, in my neck of the woods."

In that case I'll be kind to your readers, if that's all they want to know, tell them I don't know, because people like you, wont let me forget the horrible things that happen to me.

He sat and looks at me; I could see he was thinking should he ask another question.

Well if you have to write something 'Nick, write the truth, and "don't" find me guilty again.

'Nick, you and I went to the same school infant school, you know me from way back, so if you write anything that is not said at this table, I will be after you with law, and you know I will win.

'So you see you don't need 'Jim, to come after you, so be a good boy, and let us have a quiet evening out."

"How long are you here for?" Just the weekend, will you have dinner with me tomorrow? "No 'Nick, I am engage."

"May I ask who the lucky man is?" You may but the answer is I will only say when I am ready.

He did not ask he anymore questions after that, he just looks at me for a while hoping I would say something.

Don't ask me 'Nick, I don't know, I just got out of prison, and I am having a quiet drink with my lawyer.

"Good luck 'Jim."

"Lisa, enjoy your night out, he said and walk away.

She looks at me waiting for me to react, to what he said. I said nothing.

'Jim, don't let it worry you, I will explain later." There is nothing to explain, you did what you thought was right, so I am not worried.

'You are "innocent" so no matter what they write, or say it will not harm me."

You did not tell me you are engage.

"If I told you would you go out with me?" Yes so when are you going to ask me to marry you, you don't waste time do you? "Why should I, sooner or later it will come out that you are shacking up with me, we can't hide it from them, all of our life, can we? "Jim let's not worry about it now, let's enjoy the evening, we have a lot of time to talk about it."

"I know I have a lot to explain to you but believe me it's alright."

You want to know something you are so elegant and smart in the courts, out here with me you drop it all, but you still use it to your advantage, in a different way.

'Jim, when I see what I want, I have news for you I will use everything at my disposal to get it, and that goes for you."

"I fell in love with you and I waited three long years for you," and I am going to try my best not to loose you now, does that answer your question?" Yes. "Good, so would you like another drink?" After a while all her friends, and all the nosey parkers as she call them, stop asking questions.

I said nothing for quite a while, "are you all right she asks?" I am fine.

"Well if you are, please come back to me; I am feeling "lonely" sitting here by myself.'

I was thinking about finding a job.

'Jim lets talk about this tomorrow, let's enjoy our first night out together, 'don't' worry about that now I have everything under control."

Let's have another drink, don't listen to daddy, he would ask you to go to work right now, I don't want you to.

146

'We'll go for a drive tomorrow; I have something I want to show you so let's enjoy the evening,' and if you promise me you will be a good boy, I'll let you walk me home down the country lane." You are joking? "I never joke about the country lane; she said smiling I always walk that way home, so if you are nice I will let you walk me home, and I mean it."

When we got home her mom was waiting for us. "Did you enjoy yourself?" Yes thanks. "Do you want something to eat?" No thanks Mom.

"Okay" good night then." Good night Mom.

I will get something for myself Mom, "good night then, see you in the morning." Good night Mom."

Next morning 'Lisa was up early she bought me a cup of tea, rub my head morning wakie, wakie get up now Mom's getting breakfast hurry up."

I try to grab her; "oh, no you don't and hurry out the door."

We had breakfast and went for a drive, we drove for about an hour and a half, when she said we are here, we turn into a drive way.

"What do you think of that she said?" What I said.

"The house and look at the scenery." That is very nice, it is beautiful.

"I bought it just over a year now," I could not refuse it;" it was a killing."

What are you going to do with it? "I am thinking of turning it into a holiday lodge, a lot of people go hiking here, I come here myself, once a year."

There are very few places to stay in, in this area; I got planning permission to build all ready; I look into it before I bought the place, my plan is to plant a lot of trees, to hide the buildings when you are above.

That sounds good it will change the look of the valley.

"That's why I am planting the trees to hide the buildings, that way you will only see the trees down here when you are up in the hills."

I could see the look of pride in her eyes, but why is she telling me this, it was then I remember 'Ron, with his rich girl friend, and all the advice I gave him, and how to take care of her.

Here I am looking at beauty and brains and possible money, and me with nothing, not even a job.

I sudden feel out of my dept, the feeling is this dream real? Will I wake up and find everything comes crashing down around me.

I was so far gone with my thought I did not hear everything she was saying for quite a while.

147

Then I hear her calm soothing voice calling, "Jim, are you all right, what is the matter she ask? 'Oh, nothing I said.

She gave me a hug and asks are you feeling cold?" No I am fine now.

"Are you sure?" Yes. "Would you like a hot drink?" That could be nice, we went back to the car and she pull out a flask with hot coffee, we sat in the car and drink it.

'Jim, what do you think of my plans?" It is fantastic what made you think of it? "We use to come here when I was a kid I loved it, but most of the time it was hard to find a place to stay, daddy always book in advance."

Even now if you want to spend sometime here you have to book in advance, I heard daddy say many times it would be nice, if someone would build a nice lodge, in the valley."

"I came here about a year ago and the owner said he was thinking of selling, so I ask him to give let me know when, and give me first choice."

"While I was waiting, I got a friend to check if I could build on the land, he said yes so I bought it."

The plans is been drawn up now and the work will start next year if they approve some minor changes I ask for."

Lets go and look inside, I'll keep this old building get it fix up real good, and make an office, and living quarters in the back, so if we want to come here to hike we will have everything here ready."

I was not sure I heard her say we, so I ponder over it for a while, thinking does she know what she said.

"Jim, what is the matter you seams so distance, as if you are not here, am I going two fast for you,' if I am let me know."

"Sorry I could not tell you of this when you were inside," there is so much I wish I could tell you, so don't be angry if I spring them on to you now, I love you."

At the door she gave me the keys, open the door please. "I have to go back to the car."

Do you need any help? "No just make sure the door doesn't shut behind you."

I walk around the different rooms and the kitchen and out into the back garden, when I got back she was in the lounge sat on a settee with the fire on.

"What do you think of it?" It is very nice, it will need a lot of work to renovate it; "I know I look into what it will cost already."

There is ninety-five acres of land, I am going to build a riding stable, so people can come here on riding holidays, there is a river, I'll clear it and stock it with fish, so anyone who want to fish, can fish."

"I am looking at everything that will make it a complete holiday area, for all kind of holidays."

She pauses for a while as if she could not find anymore to say.

Then she said lets eat, but first I have something else to show you.

She took my hand and led me to one of the bed room and pushes the door open, on the floor a blanket, and two pillows.

"Will that do she ask smiling?" Do what I ask? "You know." It will do fine but it will be awfully cold.

"Not when I get you in the mood, you will think it is eighty degrees outside."

"I can't let you get away with it; you got away last night because we were in my daddy's house, but today you are in my shack miles from anywhere."

Once again she opens the door to haven, and our world was at peace, there was just the two of us, in a cold room but this did not matter.

I gave her a kiss on the cheek and she gave me one, as our bodies went limp, but still locked, into each other.

Are you all right now I ask? "Yes she said you are getting better at it."

"Well I suppose I better get you something to eat," to build up your strength for next time," she said laughing and run out the door into the warmer room."

When she came back, she brought a picnic basket, full of goodies.

How early did you get up I ask? "Mom prepares it, I told her I was coming down here, she knows there are no restaurants for miles, and you can thank her when you get back." 'Lisa, my next date is with the law, you know detectives 'Gurney, and 'Bradford.

To what extend will I be involve? "Well they may want to question you; it all depends on how much evidence they have against them already."

What if they plea's guilty? "Well if they plea's guilty you may not be called."

Can I still go to the courts on the day they are tried, if they don't want me? "Why 'Jim, what do you want to do that for?" I would like to see their faces.

"It will do you no good; please don't go, please let it go now," I "don't" want to see you angry anymore," so will you stay away for me."

How long before they will call me, if they want me? "The courts decide when to set the date."

"Okay" my other case 'Brian, and 'Lonny.

"As far as I know, they plea guilty already," I heard it through the grape vine; I did not tell you this because it's not "official" yet."

What will happen to them now? "It's up to the judge; again no one knows what he will do."

My next question is the one your dad asks me. "What did he ask you?" Finding work, I have to get a job.

'Jim, enjoy your freedom for a while, don't worry about it." 'Lisa, I have nothing, only the few pounds they gave me when I leave.

"You have me so why are you worried."

I though they would give me back the three hundred pounds they took the day arrest me.

"That's an idea I'll get that for you, and I will find out what you are entitle to, and chase them for that."

"Do you really want to work?" Of course I do.

"Well I'll make you an offer, you are a very good cook, I'll hire you while you have a rest, how is that."

"I can't pay a lot, but I can make up for it in other ways."

What other way? "Sex for one, she said laughing." Well that's new, that's the first time I been paid for it.

"Oh, 'Jim, I did not mean it that way I am sorry, I was only joking sorry."

Don't let it worry you, I am not, I know you were joking.

'Lisa, I enjoy sex with you so much, would you like to pay me some in advance right now. "No I don't give credit, but I'll give it to you free."

Let's go home I said. "You are a chicken she said."

Well I must save some of energy, so we can do it again for free tomorrow.

"No not tomorrow, we will do it again tonight as soon as I get home."

"Let's be serious 'Jim, I don't want you to go back to work not just yet, I am working on something so wait and see, if I get it first, will you please." Okay.

"Would you like to drive?" Yea that would be nice, I have not driven for a long time do you trust me with your car.

"Of course I trust you with it."

She turn the radio on push her seat back, you better direct me, remember I have never been here before.

Its easy drive straight until you see the A44 sign then turn left, if I fall a sleep wake me when you turn.

When I turn onto the A44 I woke her, we got back to her parent house, just in time for dinner.

Her Mom said I thought you were not going to make it; 'I was a sleep 'Jim, drove.'

Mom we have to leave right after dinner, if you don't mind,' I have some work to do; I am in court again tomorrow.

'That's fine; it is nice of you to come, thank you for coming also you' Jim, that's all right, Mom its nice meeting you, sorry we couldn't stay longer.

'Jim, I read 'Lisa, report on your case, I can't see where you should have anymore trouble. Thanks Mike.

"At least there is nothing that I can't sort out, with the legal system as far as I can see; I'll start on this right away.

Thank you 'Mike, can you give me an estimate how much it will cost; I won't have any money until the case is settled, and knowing my luck it will be very little, or nothing.

"We will worry about that bridge 'Jim, when we come to it.'

Thanks again Mike.

When we got home 'Lisa, got stuck in her work, and I start to read my books again, after a while I kiss her on the neck and went to bed.

"I'll be up as soon as I finish this she said."

I was fast asleep by the time she came to bed, and when she went to work.

Around 10:00 o'clock the phone rang, so you are awake, you was snoring your head off last night, you sure had a good night sleep.

Thank you for not waking me.

"That okay it's nice to see you are settling down.'"

"Jim, look out side."

I look out side through the window there is a new car out there.

"It's yours she said, if you "don't" like the colour tell them to change it."

"The keys should be on the floor down stairs by the front door."

"Come for dinner I am buying," 'Lisa, what are you trying to do to me? "What do you mean?" Are you trying to give me a heart attack? "No I am

151

just making sure you can get around, in stead of stuck in the house all the time."

'Lisa, saying thanks is not enough. "Jim, all I ask in return is your love and for that everything I have is yours."

I said nothing for a long time, are you still there she asks?" Yes.

'What's the matter?" Nothing I am fine. "Are you sure?" Yes I am sure. "Will I see you for dinner?" Yes. "Bye then sees you."

At dinner, "I have some good news for you," she said."

What more good news? That's nice.

"You can pick up your three hundred pounds, anytime you want."

'That's" not all 'Gurney, and 'Bradford, plea guilty at the hearing a few hours ago.

"They will be sentencing them, on Monday 20 June at the 3:00pm."

'Jim, I am going to ask you, to stay away, please get it out of your system will you please."

"I don't think it will help you going back, to hear all the horrible things that was done to you."

I sat there, I said nothing; I scratch my head and rub my eyes and cover them with my hand, to hide the tears in my eyes.

She grabs my wrist across the table and whisper I love you, then hand me a "tissue."

I dry my eyes and look at her and whisper back I love you, thanks for everything, you are welcome she said with a smile.

"Let's eat; I have to get back to work."

Do you want me to cook for when you get home? "No unless you feel like another cook meal?" No not really.

"Well we will eat what we can find, or send out for something."

"Jim, I have this case and another next month; I have nothing else for the next two months, so how about going away for a good holiday in the sun somewhere."

"You choose where you would like to go."

"How about going to see your parents for a few weeks, and then have a couple more to our self, somewhere it's nice and quiet."

That sounds good. "Okay' I'll get it book up, as soon as you decide."

What, if the court wants me when they have the hearing for detective 'Gurney, and 'Bradford.

"Oh, that's will be some time yet, we should be back by then, don't worry about that, I'll be in contact with daddy every day."

Once again I remember 'Ron, when I was driving home; as soon as I get home I must ring him.

As I walk into the house the phone start ringing.

Hello Jim the voice said, it's 'Mike, 'Mike, 'Mike who I said? You know, 'Lisa's dad, I am sorry sir; I did not recognise your voice. "That's okay."

"I am just calling to tell you the news about detective Gurney," thank you 'Mike.

'Lisa told me 'oh, good, thought she was in court today?" She is we had dinner.

I just walk in as the phone rang.

I have to see you, will you make an appointment, to see me one day next week.

Okay 'Mike, ill do that, bye. Bye 'Mike.

I hang up the phone and walk into the kitchen to get a drink, and then I remember 'Ron, I must call him, now, before I forget.

"Hello 'Jim, I thought you would forget me now you are free."

"When I did not hear from you, I said to myself he won't remember me, because of the bad memories that go with this place."

'Ron no such luck, if it was not for you, I would have found a way to hang myself, or some other way of ending my life.

"What is it like to be free?" 'Ron, do you really want to know? "Of course I want to know, he said in his grammar school accent."

Well I said you will have to wait, I don't want to spoil the surprise you will get, when you walk out the gates."

Are you still getting married? "Yes as soon as I get out of here we will set a date; don't forget you promise me you will come."

I always keep my promise. "Thanks 'Jim."

Then he asks the question I know he would ask. "How many women you been out with since you leave here?" 'Ron, it is none of your business.

"Come on 'Jim, he said, you are not woman shy are you?" Yea I am.

"You lie I don't believe you," come on spill the beans.

Okay 'Ron, just one. "That's a start he said."

Ron, I found the one I want.

"That's good, does she have money?" I don't know, I haven't asked her, and I don't care if she have money are not.

He went quiet for a while, as if he ran out of questions.

Then he said have you been to bed with her yet?" Ron it's none of your business.

"Sorry he said that's a touchy subject he said laughing."

And then he commented "I just want to know if you use those shinny balls of yours yet."

'Ron, it is still none of your business.

"Where did you meet her?" 'Ron, lets talk about something else.

When will they let you out? "In another five weeks I hope."

Okay I'll pop in to see you, next week.

"Are you sure?" Yea, 'see you then.' Okay see you bye.

When 'Lisa, got home I told her about 'Ron, and what he did for me, I told her I was going to visit him.

"She said jokingly whatever you do don't get yourself lock up again will you"

"I don't know what I would do without you now."

Joking I said find another man.

"How do I know he is going to satisfy me she asks?" Well you have to try him, and if it "doesn't" work you will just have to go without won't you I said.

"Jim you are wicked, I am sure you don't mean it."

I told her 'Ron is getting "married" as soon as he is out, and that we are invited.

"What is he in side for she asks?" What did you say I ask? "What did he do for them to lock him up she ask?" Con women, his girl friend is very rich.

"What is her name she asks?" 'Dee, 'that's' all I know, I don't know her last name or his.

"I know her, and I know 'Ron, we went to the same infant school, her name is 'Dee Luton, and his is 'Ron Singleton."

"You really mean she is getting married to him?" 'That's' what he told me.

"She took him back, I can't believe that," I cannot see that marriage lasting for long," he is two wild, every woman he see he think he should go to bed with them."

"She is crazy, mind you; she was crazy about him from school days," they were always together, until her parents send her to an all girl school.

"I cannot see what she sees in him." I thought that my self when I saw her photograph I thought she must be blind.

She has a son for him that could be the reason she is having him back.

Well the only thing I can say is you know him, that's 'Ron, alright.

"How much did you get to know him?" We share a cell all the time I was there, he told me about his life style.

So I ask what the hell he was doing to himself and 'Dee? And that's when he sat down and listens to me, and rang her.

She told him she had a kid for him, now they are super glued together. I hope I haven't done something wrong.

"No I don't think so, I am sure if you did not say anything, when he got out she would go after him again, that's how she is.

As far as she is concern he can't do any wrong.

Three years seems a long time for conning her. "Is that what he told you?" Yes.

"Well it was not just her, there was two other women involve.

If it was just 'Dee, they would only given him six months maybe nine months, but he was making a career of conning women.

I remember the case he took fifteen thousand off them, before they caught him.

"Would you like a drink?" Yes I'll get. "No I'll get it."

"What would you like?" Anything, what you are drinking will do.

She got the drink came back and sits down beside me; 'I hope 'Ron did not teach you anything of his tricks." What do you mean? "How to chase women for starters, let's be honest can you see him teaching me anything? "No not really."

Well let's talk about something else, your dad rang today, he told me what you told me, about 'Gurney, pleading guilty.

I told him you ask me not to go to the hearing, he agrees with you, but I still have reservations, so I will deal with it when the day comes.

He wants to see me one day next week, he did not say what he wanted to discuss.

"I don't know, he did not tell me either," don't worry it will only be something, he doesn't want to talk about on the phone, or he wants you to sign something.

"How did you like the car?" I love it, I kiss her on the forehead, is that the best you can do.

No I thought you are tired, would you like another drink I ask? 'Yes please, I will have the same."

By the time I got back to her, she went to her desk and start working.

As I start reading my books, and trying to get some work ready to send, I stop and just stare at the books.

"How are you getting on she ask?" Struggling a bit now it's getting harder.

"I will check the collage to see if you can enrol in evening class, if that is all right with you." That could be good, I think it would help.

When, I went to see 'Mike, he told me that he is going for the maximum amount he can get from the "government."

"You will win, but how much you'll get, that's what we have to work on."

Okay 'Mike, I leave it with you; "you are very trusting aren't you?" Well, let's put it this way, if I can't trust you 'Mike, who I can trust.

"What are you doing with your time now?" Nothing yet, I told 'Lisa, I should find a job, but she still think that I should, have a break first and decide what I want to do, so I spend my time studying.

"I think that is a good idea, but if you leave it two long you will find it hard to get back into the system."

"If there is anything I can do for you when you are ready, don't be afraid to ask."

Okay 'Mike, I will remember your offer, thank you.

I have a problem; I know you and 'Lisa, think I should not go to the hearing of detective 'Gurney, and 'Bradford, that I should put the whole thing behind me.

'Lisa, think I should stay away, because it will upset me hearing all the unpleasant things again, but I want to see their faces when the judge sentences them.

I know this is the only way that I will be satisfied and possible have a closer.

I want to see their face when they hear the sentence.

'Jim, I think you are wrong but if that is the way you feel you can get a closure you must go.

My problem is how I tell 'Lisa. 'Jim, 'Lisa, will understand if you explain it to her as you explain it to me.

"What about the other hearings, do you intend to go to them also?" Yes, from the expression on his face, I could see he was, not sure I should.

"Jim, there could be a lot of new evidence describing what they did to you, that you haven't heard are can't remember, they could be very explicit," hearing them could do more harm than good.

156

"Mike, it's a part of my life I have to see it right through to the end, no matter what they have to say, it's a part of my life I know I will never forget, because there was so much filth back there.

So I feel the only way I can put an end to it, is to see it right through to the end, no matter what.

There are nights when I think it was my fault why they did what they did, just because I don't know the full story.

They knock me out, so all I can remember is the first few minutes.

"Jim, now that you explain it like that, I understand, and I am sure 'Lisa, will understand also, but believe me you won't like some of the things you will hear."

That afternoon when I got home I turn on the TV news it said detective 'Gurney, died suddenly of a suspected heart attack.

His wife said he complain of acid indigestion and a slight chest pain, just before we went to bed," then he woke up about 2:30 this morning with a severe chest pain, and died on the way to hospital.

Detective, 'Gurney was suspended eleven weeks ago; for beating detainees to get convictions.

His most publicize case is that of 'Mr Jim Sears, known as the nut cracker, who was arrested and found guilty of robbery with a machete.

He was sentence to six years by 'Judge Wilson, and served three years, for a crime he did not do.

'Mr Sears was beaten badly, when he was arrested, by detective 'Gurney, and detective 'Bradford, his partner at the time.

Detective Bradford is also suspension.

Detective 'Gurney, was hit very hard in his private by 'Mr Jim Sears, when he was in the interrogation room.

Because of that blow, detective 'Gurney lost one of his testicles, and "Mr Jim Sear suffered a crack skull and two broken ribs, in that incidence.

Eight weeks ago 'Detective Gurney, and detective 'Bradford, pleads guilty to assaulting 'Mr Jim Sears, they are a waiting sentencing.

I turn the TV, off with disgust; I could not believe the son of a bitch took the easy way out, he cheated me, out of seeing his face with the hand cuffs on, being lead away through the door.

I was looking forward to see the look on the bastard's face when I wave him good bye.

"That evening when 'Lisa, got home the first thing she said I love you."

"Sit, I have some news for you, big foot 'Gurney, is dead."

157

I know I saw it on the news, he took the easy out he cheated me I wanted to see his face when they take him away.

I was still mad, but I try my best not to show it because I did not want to upset her.

But I am sure she could see from the expression on my face, I was not pleased.

Next day I went to see 'Ron, when I enter the visitor's gate my heart skip a beat.

'Ron was in the visitor's room waiting.

His first words were, "what is it like to be free, when are you coming back?" He asks jokingly. So I said I would come back tomorrow if you ask me.

"Why tomorrow he ask?" Well it's a bit late to book in today; we had a little giggle about that.

How is 'Dee, and little 'Ron? "Man she can't wait for me to get out; she will have every thing ready for the wedding, as soon as I walk through the gates," so you will be getting your invitation when we decide on the date."

"She will be sending invitations to most of her school friends."

I have a shock for you; my lawyer knows you and 'Dee, she said they went to the same school.

"What is your lawyer's name?" 'Lisa. "You don't mean 'Lisa Myrna?" Yes. "I know her; she was voted the girl most likely to succeed and she did, she turned out to be a big time lawyer, how could you afford her?" You don't want to know its long story.

"We use to call her the book worm; we also call her the "eternal" virgin, because if a boy just touches her she got mad.

Hold on I said before you say anymore.

He looks at me, and pause then it hit him like a brick. "Your lawyer, you always talk about her, you jammy sod he said, you are one lucky sod. 'Man every boy in school tries to take her out including me," she looks at us, like we were a piece of shit; she was so sure of herself in everything she did."

This is good news wait until I tell 'Dee, she will be over the moon, we knew she went into her father's law practice, but we did not keep in touch.

She is always in the papers; 'she takes only the big money cases, how did you get her to take yours?" 'Ron, it's a long story, all I can tell you she volunteer. "So you found yourself a rich one."

Who told you she is rich? 'Jim, she is not short of a penny, you will be alright."

The truth is 'Ron, I never thought about it, rich or poor.

I would still go for her, man she is a cracker, she is a dream come true for me," but to tell you the truth I am so busy trying to sort my life out, I don't have time to think of her money.

So if she is rich good luck to her, it's not mine I am sorry to say, and I won't be doing what you did.

'Ron, I am sorry I should not have said that.

That's all right 'Jim, you are right I was bloody stupid, and I know it now, so don't apologize.

Man do you want to know something else; I ask myself everyday what does she want me for? Is she only playing with me, until she gets fed- up? "Well 'Jim, you will have to wait and see, but I can tell you this, 'Lisa is not the type to play with anything.

"She is a one man woman; she is the type that goes for what she wants, and gets it."

'Jim, can I ask a question, have she bought you anything yet?" Yes she has.

'Is it expensive?' Yes it is.

"Well what is it?' She bought me some clothes and a new car.

"Is it a brand new car?" Yes.

'Jim, did you ask her for any of the stuff?" No, she bought them without telling me.

"Well what more do you want; she is telling you she loves you her way."

"Come on 'Jim, what more do you want her to do?" 'Ron, I have never been treated like this way before.

"Well get use to it, take a leaf out of the book that you use to tell me how to treat 'Dee," and read it your self."

'I thank you for that; man you made me sees how stupid I was," one thing for sure I am the luckiest man in the world now."

"One last question, have you met her parents?" Yes.

"Did you ask to meet them?" No.

"Well you better watch it you're on your way down the isle, my friend," 'Jim; you are screwed that's for sure, if you don't want her, you better run now," or do something stupid like I did, take her money and end up in here."

How long do you have to do now? "I don't really know they should let me out anytime now, the sooner the better," believe me I learn a lesson I did not need."

Are you alone in the cell? 'No, I have a new cell mate, his name 'Jack, he is an asshole; he is a real little softie,' he cries every night."

"If you want I can kick him out so you can come back."

'Ron you, want to know something? I "don't" like you that much.

"Thank you, I thought you were my friend."

Who needs friends like you if you want to lock me up again? 'Maybe you are right," because I would not come back for you either."

Well that proves you don't like me that much either.

"Jim, I am glad I met you, you change my life."

'Ron, I am glad I met you also, there were nights back there I did not think I was going to walk out of that cell.

"Have you heard anything about 'Brian and 'Lonny? Yes, they plea guilty so they will be spending some more time in here, or some where else soon.

"Jim, can I ask you this now, what did you do to 'Gurney?" Man that was one hell of a punch; I hit the bastard so hard it crushes one of his nuts.

The doctor said when I hit him, I hit him upwards and his testacies got crush on his pelvis bone.

I heard something about that; they remove his nut because it was crushed, yes I remember hearing it in side the police station, before I came in here.

"So it was you, no wander you are famous."

I though 'Jerry, would tell you, that I was the one who spoil 'Gurney's night life.

"Jim, 'Jerry is so afraid of you," if I ask him to spell your name he would pass out."

"He told me about the first time he meet you, how you tell him to go and have a shower."

"He told me you did not threaten him, that your look was enough, when you ask him."

"About the 'Boss, what did he do for you?" 'Ron, I can't tell you so forget it; you are still inside here, and the less you know the better off you will be.

You said to me once, when I ask you about him, the less I know about him the better off I will be, well I am saying the same to you now.

"Its funny they still talk about you in here."

"The joke is if anyone steps out of line, they say, I'll send for the nut cracker to crack your nuts."

"How, is the news people, treating you?" Well let's put it this way they leave me alone so far, because they don't know where to find me.

The first day I thought I was going to have some trouble, one was out side waiting for me, I told him news writers are nothing but liars.

That everything they wrote about me, when I was taken in was lies, so I warn him to stay away from me, if he doesn't want to see mad.

Maybe it's because they can't find me, why you can't read anything about me.

'Take a tip 'Jim, keep your hands to yourself, walk away no matter what they say, use the law instead, you don't want to do something stupid now you are free."

"If they come after you just say you don't have a story, because you are going to write a book, and you need the story for yourself."

'Ron, do you want to know something you are a genius.

"Thank you 'Jim, I did not know I was that good."

What I mean is sometime you talk a lot of rubbish, but this time you make sense.

"I make sense?" Yes. "What did I say?" You mean you "don't" know? "If I knew I wouldn't be asking you would I?" 'Ron, you said to tell the "reporters" that I don't have a story because I will need it for the booking writing.

"Jim, I am brilliant aren't I?" You know what it is so good; I did not need to think about what I said, I just say it."

'Ron, you better stop thinking now before your brain seize up. 'Ha, 'ha, very funny."

But let's put fun and joke aside, it is a brilliant idea, and I will use it, when I get home I am going to get me a type writer, and write about me.

'Jim, buy your self a computer.'

I don't know anything about computers.

"You don't know anything about writing either do you?" 'It will take you a while but if you stick to it, it is possible you will write a best seller."

Well 'Ron, I have to leave you, it's been nice seeing you again, I hope the next time I see you, you are out side, and then you can tell me what it's like to be free.

Here is my number give me a ring as soon as you get out, but don't give this number to anyone, because it's not mine.

'I'll ring you as soon as I set my foot out side the gates.' Do that.

Bye 'Jim, Bye 'Ron. See you.

When I got home, 'Lisa was home and she started the cooking. As soon as I enter the door she came out and give me a hug and kiss, it was as if we were parted for a long time.

Jokingly she said I thought they kept you again.

Well I am sorry to disappoint you they don't want me anymore, I try my best to get back in, but they slam the door in my face.

'Ha, 'ha, very funny. Then she ran off shouting my cooking.

I follow her into the kitchen and kiss her on the back of her neck, she turn a round and give me a little peck on my cheek.

Drink she ask? Yea, 'wine or beer,' I'll get it, what you are cooking? "Wait and see." Whatever it is it smells good.

I am sorry I did not get home in time to cook for you.

"That's no problem; let me surprise you for a change, so I can prove I am not just a pretty face."

"Did you enjoy yourself?" Not really, I was worried they would not let me out all the time I was there.

I told 'Ron, about you, he remembers you; he said you went to the same infant school.

"So what else did he have to say about me?" He said you were a cracker, and that you were a book worm, voted the girl most likely to succeed.

"Is that all?" Yes.

"What he did not tell you how I slap his face, for grabbing my butt when I was twelve?" No he did not tell me.

"Jim, I hit him so hard, my arm hurt for days."

"I did not know you could hit?" "Boys should not touch.' I touch.

"That's different."

How is that different? "Well let's say you are old enough, and I say you can."

"You honestly mean he did not tell you I hit him?" No, maybe he forgot.

"That is impossible I hit him so hard I almost took his head off."

"Well the only thing I can say he is afraid that you will hurt his pride and joy, because there is no way he could forget it, not in a life time."

Well it seams to me you took care of the problem when you slap him, but if he tries it again let me know.

"Jim, I don't think so."

Why? "Because I love you two much, I don't want to see you angry again in my life time.

I took my beer into the sitting room, and turn on the television and sit on the settee, she follow me and sit on my lap, and put he tongue in my ear.

"Then whisper in my ear, dinner will be ready in thirty five minutes."
That's nice, good I am hungry. "We have thirty five minutes."
What for I ask? "Do you want me to spell it out?" Yes. 'Can I play with 'Jim? Who is 'Jim? "Your tool as you calls it." Why do you want to do a thing like that? 'Because I want to play with him right now, I have been waiting all day."

Do you always get what you want? "Yes." Well go a head and play with him.

You want to know something 'Lisa, you are one in a million.

'Jim, why you are telling me something I know what are you after?" I just give you something I "cherish" very much."

Only because it was itching and you needed me to scratch it for you.

"No it was not itching." Yes it was.

"Jim, I am the lawyer and I know when I itch."

You use Jim's tool to scratch your itch, and what you did to Jim it is not funny.

Did you know you just murder 'Jim's tool, look it is dead as a door nail,' you are a wicked woman, why don't you admit you need me to scratch your itch, and say you are sorry you use my tool to scratch it.

'Ha, poor 'Jim, I busted his tool and I did not hear him scream."

You did not give him time to scream did you? "Why should I, when 'Jim, just stand there and enjoy it."

Well baby if you keep playing with 'Jim's tool you will get a little 'Jim, to look after, because 'Jim, will never run away.

"Ha, well that is nice to know."

What will your mother and father say when you tell them? "Tell them what?"

That you play with 'Jim's tool and you are in trouble? "Why should they say anything, I am a big girl now, and I am the one that will be having it, and I am old enough to, and I know what I want.'

'Jim, would you like to hear something funny?" Yes please, I could do with a laugh right now.

"You will be the one at home looking after little 'Jim," he or she will have a daddy, at home for a mommy." 'Ha, 'ha, that is very funny.

Well, we will cross that bridge when we get to it.

"Does that mean you don't mind?" 'Lisa, what are you cooking? 'You can't feed him yet, he is not old enough."

What is the matter with you? How much have you had to drink? I thought you were cooking.

"Oh, hick I forget, it's a good thing I turn the heat down before you had your evil way with me."

Now I know you had a lot to drink.

Should I finish cooking for you? "No it should be ready now; you can lay the table while I make the gravy if you want to help."

I hope it's not burnt, I don't like burnt food, and I have to eat to get ready for the next time.

"Jim, who told you there will be a next time?" Well let's put it this way, I 'don't' need anybody to tell me.

I know there will be a next time, because you can't walk away from a good thing.

'Jim, what good thing are you talking about?" You are in a funny mood today let's, eat please it will be my first meal today.

"What are you trying to do to yourself; not eating is bad for you, and having sex without eating is bad for you also."

"What are you trying to do, are you trying to be the thinnest man in the country?" Not really, I just forget to eat.

"What are you doing tomorrow?" I "don't" know. "Come and have dinner with me; I promise I will leave 'Jim, alone, until I get home."

Okay I'll be there, I like free food, and I love every minute I spend with you even if we are in a restaurant, so that means I will have two things I like in the same place.

'Lisa, we have to have to talk, "you sound serious?" Yes.

"Let's eat first okay."

Okay after we eat I'll wash up, you been at work all day.

"I'll dry and we both can sit down at the same time."

As we sat down she asks? "What do you want to talk about?" I "don't" know how to put this.' 'Jim, just say it."

"Okay, I feel strange having to take everything from you. "Why?" If I was you I would not let it worry me, so "don't" let it worry you."

"I will open an account for you, so you can, buy what you want."

'Lisa no, 'Jim, it's all right I want you to have your own account, this way you wont feel like you're taking it off me."

"Jim, with you doing the house work for me and a few other things, you will have your hands full so you will earn what I put in the account."

What other things are you talking about? "Well you could check the lodge for me; if you take that over we won't have to hire someone."

"You see 'Jim, with you running it for us, I know it will be in safe hands."

I sat there very quiet saying nothing.

"She shakes me, wake up; it's not time to sleep yet."

I smile but said nothing for a while.

'Lisa, I don't know anything a bout running a lodge. 'Jim, I don't either so don't let it worry you, we will be working together, everything we do is ours, so if we make a mistake it will be our mistake, because I have never ran a lodge before either."

"We can learn how to run it together, just like anything else, by trial and error."

Again I sat quiet, she push me again what is the matter she ask? This is happen two fast for me to grasp, that's the matter.

"You will handle it I know you can, I am sure you can."

Again she said I will be there with you.

'Jim, last but not least, you have to look after me she said smiling, is that okay with you she asks."

I have to think about it. "What looking after me?" Do you have to think about looking after me?" Well 'Jim, I promise you that will be the best part of the job, she said smiling, I am sure you will enjoy it."

Well if you put it like that, I will try my best to satisfy you.

"Well that is good enough for me."

When I get my compensation you will have to find something to do with it, put it into your holiday camp, or invest it because I "don't" have any idea what to do with it yet.

'Jim, it's not my holiday camp it's ours.'

I been working on this holiday camp for a year and nine months, this is for you and me.

Suddenly my heart leap into my throat, I was not dreaming, I did not know what to say.

I sat there with her head in my lap and look down into her eyes.

She reaches up and strokes my cheek then she said it again.

It's for you and I, so let your compensation, stay in the bank for a while, when you get it, we will find something to do with it someday.

Six weeks later we went on holidays and we had a very nice time.

When we came back, we got the invitation to 'Ron, and 'Dee's, wedding.

Also among the letters there were two from the courts one to attend the hearing of detective 'Bradford, and the other, for 'Brian, Lonny, and Stan, hearing.

The hearing for detective 'Bradford, was very short, he was given six months suspension, and kept his job.

Judge 'Bailey, said he was only helping a fellow officer, who was in trouble.

I could not believe what I was hearing; he stood there and watches 'Gurney beat the crap out of me, and then he cracks my skull, and all he got is six month suspension.

He did not even try to stop 'Gurney, all he did is stood there and watch the son of a bitch.

I was that mad I fond it very hard to sit in my seat.

Mike, wrote on a piece of paper don't say anything; there is nothing we can do. 'Lisa must have said something to him about me loosing my cool.

So I sat there and suffer, and watch 'Bradford, walk free, I though if that is justice, Judge 'Bailey, you can stick it up his ass.

Three days later I was back in court again.

'Brian and 'Lonny were sitting together with two guards each, and 'Stan was sitting on the other side of the court room under guard.

Call, doctor 'Joe Wilson to the stand please, "Doctor, can you tell the court what injuries 'Jim Sears, suffered when he was attacked 'Mike asks? He had three broken ribs, broken arm, fractured jaw, two black eyes, and siemens in his mouth and both ears and all over his face, also in his rectum, he was badly beaten a round his private area and they urinate on him; they also did a number two on his chest.

"Doctor what you mean when you say they did a number two on him." 'Mike, ask? "I mean someone shit on his chest."

"He was repeatedly raped, Mike repeat?" Yes sir.

Doctor in you opinion was he beaten when he was conscious, or did they continue beating him after he pass-out.

"In opinion he was not conscious after the first few blows," but I think every time he starts to come round he was hit again to keep him quiet."

I sat there for two days listening to all the nasty crap they say happen and wonder what Judge Taylor will do to them.

As far as I was concern, the best think he could do for me, is give all

166

three of them to me so I can finish the job I started, including cutting their throat.

All I was interested in now was the verdict, and when that came I was also disappointed, 'Brian, and 'Lonny, got nine months each.

And 'Stan, got one year, and walk away with his nuts and eye, the son of a bitch, you lucky bastard I whisper, and Mike heard me.

When it was over 'Mike, said, they can't sue you." So it's over? "Yes it is."

"You may not be satisfied with the verdict after what they done to you, but for 'Lisa, sake put it behind you please."

Okay 'Mike, thank you, I don't know when I will be able to pay you.

"That's okay it's on the house." Thank you that's very kind of you.

At 'Ron, and 'Dee's, wedding I notice 'Lisa, was not eating or drinking much, and she was looked a little pale.

Are you all right I ask? I am fine she said, do you want to go home? "No, I am all right, don't worry."

She spent a lot of time talking to 'Dee, every now and again they would laugh out very loud.

"Ron said to me I bet she is telling 'Dee, about you."

Why me? "I have a feeling that's why they are laughing."

"So 'Gurney, the son of a bitch snuffs it, he took the easy way out."

'Ron, the fucker cheat me out of seeing him with hand cuff going thought the door.

"Jim, at least you have the satisfaction of taking one of his nuts that is better than nothing," plus you know that while waiting for the courts to sentence him, the bastard heart could not take it," he must have had a lot of sleepless nights.

"Look at it this way you done all new detainees a favour, putting him under pressure, that's for sure."

Ron you know what, I would have loved to see? "What?" I would have been the happiest person alive, if I was standing over him and watch him blow his fuse.

We stop talking about 'Gurney, when Lisa and 'Dee joined us.

Then 'Dee took me to one side, 'Jim, thank you she said, for having a man to man talk with 'Ron, he told me what you said to him.

He is a different person now; you must have given him a good telling off.

'Dee, I told him its time he grew up, that's all I did.

"Well he took notice of it he is a different person now, since he came out, there is not a day that he don't talks about you, he talks so much, about you I thought you must be nine feet tall." 'Ha, well I hope I done some good.

"I don't know what you do to people, but what ever it is it works," because all 'Lisa, done since she come in here is talk about you all evening; she is another one that fined you interesting.

I have known 'Lisa, for years, I never seen her with a man before, I thought she was man shy, and she would end up an old maid, but I can tell you this she is crazy about you, don't tell her I tell you."

"One thing for sure, she is not shy in the courtroom, she and her father is the best lawyer in the country."

"At school everyone knew what she was going to do when she leave school, she always say, I am going to be a lawyer if you ask."

That is from about the age of nine, she wanted nothing else.

On our way home 'Lisa, was very quiet, then she said please stop the car, she got out and sick on the side of the road.

I thought she must have eaten something that up-set her.

"When she got back in the car then she said hold on a while please."

So we sat there for quite a while talking, then she opens the door and sick again, what have you eat, I ask.

Nothing she said then closes the door.

"I am going to kill you she said in a quiet voice." Why what have I done.

And then she hit me with the bomb.

"I think I am pregnant."

I shout are you sure? Yes she said very quiet, so quiet I could hardly hear her.

Well you can't say, I did not warn you about playing with 'Jim's tool.

Jim's tool been lying around for three years and what did you do, you pick it up and start playing with it, you are a brave woman.

"Hurry up let's get home so I can murder 'Jim, and his tool, she said smiling.

Then after a long pause she said, I thought you would be angry, almost in a whisper.

Why should I be angry? "I don't know."

Are you sorry I ask? "Me no she said, I am happy," but I was worried about you," you just got your freedom and lumbered with a family." 'Lisa, the only thing I am sorry about is I can't afford a kid right now, so tomorrow I must get up off my backside and find a job.

"No 'Jim, everything stay the same, you have a whole lot of work coming your way."

"Lets talk about this later, don't let it worry you," just be there for me, that's all I want."

I start to ask her what kind of work, 'Jim, lets get home please; there is no need to worry."

"I feel like I want to sick again, could you stop please."

Thinking back on one of our conversation I remember her saying if I have a baby you will be the one looking after it.

"Ha" well I thought what the heck, I can be a daddy at home it's only a baby it can't kill me.